The Year Before Hope

a novel by

ANGELA K. HENERY

First published by Westland Publishing 2026

First edition

ISBN: 979-8-218-91874-31

Library of Congress Control Number: 2026901499

To every mother with a heavy heart and empty arms, and to every silent prayer whispered over a blank test strip. You are not alone.

Hope awaits.

Content Note

This novel addresses sensitive topics, including infertility, pregnancy loss, and grief. These experiences are portrayed with care and honesty as part of a larger story about love, resilience, and the long road toward healing.

Please take care while reading.

From a Journal

December 24, 2006

I made it home a few days ago, and it is a relief to escape the sterile hospital air. Home isn't quite the same these days. Arrangements have been made for what is to come – a constant reminder that time is not on my side.

At least I get to spend Christmas with Leslie and Taylor. I don't have the energy to make it magical like I used to, but hearing their voices down the hall is a balm to my soul. Bradley is growing weary. I see the pain etched in his face when he thinks I'm not looking. I love him endlessly, but I fear he will fade away. The girls will need him in the long months ahead.

Leslie has a strong spirit, and joy follows her like a lost puppy. She's young enough that she may only remember glimpses of me. But Taylor...

She has the biggest heart I've ever known. She taught me more about love than I ever taught her. I hope she never forgets who she is. If she ever loses her way, I pray there's someone who brings her back to the light.

Chapter 1

Flames lick up my spine. Tossing back the covers, I race to the adjoining bathroom as the familiar heat envelops me. I dunk my head under the faucet and run water over my face, taking large gulps from the stream to loosen the knot in my throat.

The scorching continues as I reach for the hem of my tank top and rip the material over my head. I cup my hands under the tap and splash the water against my bare chest, desperate to cool my heated core.

After a few minutes, the flames burn down to embers, and I'm left shivering. I turn off the tap and pluck my terry cloth robe from a nearby hook. I slip through the bedroom and down the hallway.

I hear the low drone of the TV as I enter the living room. Fireworks crackle across the screen, and cheers fill the otherwise quiet space. Apparently, Spencer didn't make it to midnight. I spot my husband fast asleep in his recliner, head lolling to the side, mouth slightly ajar.

An aftershock of warmth tingles along my skin like the

fading edge of the hot flash.

"Well. Happy fucking New Year, Taylor," I mutter to myself.

I make my way to the kitchen and pour myself a glass of ice water. Plopping into a bar stool, I drain the glass as the last of the heat subsides.

Three more days of this misery.

I burrow my head into my hands and stifle a groan. I'm getting particularly sick of this crap. It has been five years, and I'm still not a mom.

For the first three, I dealt with it silently on my own. It was fine. We weren't actively trying yet, but we weren't doing anything to prevent it either. Regardless, my fear was growing with each passing year. Then Spencer and I had "the talk" — the one where he told me he was ready to be a father, and I reluctantly agreed it was time to seek help.

Enter Dr. Hatfield, a ferret of a man in his late fifties with narrow-set eyes and a sharp nose. I disliked him immediately. At my first appointment, he took one look at my chart and said, "Well, if you'd only lose a little weight, kiddo."

Gross. For a doctor to refer to a grown-ass woman as "kiddo." It still gets under my skin. His brilliant diagnosis of obesity being the underlying cause of my infertility did not help my impression of him.

But two years of following his "so-called" expert advice and I'm no closer to being a mom. Every month on the third day of my cycle, I start my round of clomiphene. And then come the five days of hell — headaches every afternoon on my drive home from work, the blazing hot flashes that hit me at random intervals throughout the day, and the flood of hormones that tamper with my emotions.

It's been six months and still no temperature spikes or

positive home pregnancy tests. I have one last round before I have to seek out a specialist or give up altogether. The next step is IVF, and it scares the shit out of me, and I doubt we could ever afford it.

If I don't get pregnant this time, it's pretty much over.

The weight of it all has strained my relationship with Spencer. Our once lively conversations have dwindled to brief snippets shared in passing. He doesn't even come to my checkups anymore. I think he's given up. He was hoping to be a dad before the age of 30. Now that deadline is quickly approaching, and we are no closer to becoming parents than we were when we started.

I feel the crushing disappointment every time I look at him, knowing I may never be able to give him his dream. I'm afraid the only thing that can pull us back together is a baby. For now, we're strangers, but it wasn't always like this. There was a time when we were young and carefree — just two teenagers in love despite a cruel world and a mountain of grief.

I met Spencer Swanson the summer before my junior year in high school. I had been relaxing on my front porch with my nose in some murder mystery when I heard him tinkering with his dad's old car. They'd just moved in across the street, and I was annoyed by all the banging and engine revving.

To this day, I'm not sure what prompted that awkward teenager to put down her novel, cross the street, and ask him to keep it down. The engine noise and repeated banging made it incredibly hard to read, I told him. Spencer just grinned and explained he was preparing the car for the annual demolition derby at the county fair, and I just stared awestruck. With ice-blue eyes and shaggy blonde hair, he resembled one of those Dukes of Hazzard boys. I was smitten.

CHAPTER 1

Although I denied it for weeks, I think we were somehow destined to be together. It took his father dying for me to realize how much he meant to me.

I'll never forget the day my dad came into my room and told me the news that Bill Swanson had passed away. I barely knew Spencer, but I understood the pain of losing a parent. I later showed up on his doorstep. Instead of greeting him or expressing my sympathy, I simply blurted, "My mom died two years ago."

I remember him nodding in silent understanding as we sat on the front stoop, wordlessly holding vigil until stars appeared above the blue spruce in my front yard.

From then on, I was a regular at the Swanson house. While his mom worked her shifts at the hospital, we did homework and watched cheesy action movies, never once discussing our shared grief.

I smile wistfully, thinking back on those early days — the long drives in the country after he won the homecoming game, stolen kisses under the bleachers after practice. It was every bit the perfect high school sweetheart story. God, I miss those two kids.

At that moment, my phone buzzes, drawing me out of my reverie.

Leslie: *I can't believe he finally asked! So excited to be Mrs. Heller!*

Along with my sister's text is a photo of a perfectly manicured hand adorned with a large glittering diamond.

Despite her happy news, an ill feeling twists in my gut. I love my sister dearly, but her fairy tale existence has always been a sticking point for me. She's my opposite in every way: young, vibrant, gorgeously blond, and untarnished by grief.

She was just a kid when Mom died. I did my best to take care of her as any big sister would. Then our dad met Geni, and everyone seemed to move on without me. While my stepmother is perfectly nice, there is no replacement for the woman who raised me. Leslie had no trouble adapting and even flourishing in our new version of family, but at 16, I was bitter and angry. Over the years, a lingering envy has hung over my relationship with her.

Right now, that shard of jealousy is digging a bit deeper.

Chapter 2

Coming back to work after the holidays is like trying to swim through peanut butter — pointless and exhausting. Half of management is still on vacation, yet my to-do list is a mile long. I barely slept after last night's hot flash, and I'm in a foul mood this morning.

"Holy buckets, Tay! Last night was fire!"

Shelby's giddy voice breaks through the buzzing static. Closing out of the spreadsheet on my screen, I swivel my chair to face my cubicle mate and best friend.

"These fine gentlemen at the Q Lounge bought us a round of drinks and offered to take us home! You totally should have been there!"

I give her a pointed look.

"Yeah, yeah, you old married lady!" She rolls her eyes at me, "But old married ladies can still come out and have a good time!"

"I think you're forgetting an adjective in there," I tell her, "I am also an old, *tired*, married lady."

She scoffs at my remark. After nearly ten years in the same

office, she's gotten used to my brand of sarcasm.

"I know, *'I'm not a club kind of girl.'* I get it," she says with air quotes.

I raise an eyebrow at her horrible imitation, "Is that really what I sound like?"

"No, you're right. It actually sounds a bit whinier."

I stifle a retort, reminding myself that I'm a grown woman and sticking my tongue out at her would be silly and childish. Instead, I choose to ignore her comment entirely.

"So," I mumble, "Leslie got engaged."

"Oh man!" Shelby snaps to attention at the thought of fresh gossip, "To that strait-laced lawyer guy, right?"

I nod my head in reply.

She wrinkles her nose, "I could never. One guy for the rest of my life? Boo!"

I give her an incredulous look, "Shelb, don't you ever see yourself settling down?"

"I don't know," she says, tucking a platinum blonde strand behind her ear, "I'm having too much fun. I'm sure your sister will live boringly ever after, but that's just not for me. At least, not right now."

I bark out a laugh, "You are the worst! Lucky for you, I love you anyway."

"You just love to live vicariously through me."

She's not entirely wrong. While on the surface, we are as different as two people can be, deep down, my work wife is everything I wish I could be. Something about Shelby Peters just draws people in. She's charismatic, bold, and a straight shooter, although perhaps a bit immature at times. She's a woman who is going places. Unlike me.

I've been in the same marketing analyst role at Apex Financial Solutions for nearly a decade. In the same amount of time, Shelby has skyrocketed from intern to senior marketing strategist. But I landed here under different circumstances.

Getting married straight out of high school has its limitations. While my Oak Hill High School classmates were getting their degrees at the universities in Lincoln or Omaha halfway across the state, I only made it an hour away from my hometown.

Denton Heights, Nebraska, isn't a busy metropolis, nor is it a Podunk little town. With a population of nearly 38,000 nestled in the central part of the state, it's the perfect size for someone like me. Big enough to be relatively anonymous, small enough that I can get across town in 20 minutes or less.

I went to the local community college, attending classes in the evening after working all day selling shoes at the mall. Spencer, who graduated the year before me, worked the night shift at Heartland Manufacturing, a plant specializing in steel shelving for grocery stores. Between classes and work, we hardly saw each other that first year. The minute I received my associate's degree in business administration, I began applying for any job I could get. The marketing analyst job at Apex seemed like a huge step up from my retail job, so I took it with zero hesitation.

The money was good, and once Spencer got put on days, it seemed like everything was finally falling into place. We were going to start the family we always talked about, and it would be happily ever after.

But between the stress of my new manager's crazy expectations and the rising anxiety about not getting pregnant, our fairy tale seemed to be waning. Maybe if I can dig myself out of the rut I'm in, we can find a way back to each other.

A warning cough sounds from one cubicle over. "Sandra's on the move," Jenna mutters just loud enough for us to hear.

We cease our banter, and I slip my headphones back over my ears and delve back into the marketing report.

Our assistant manager has a habit of making morning rounds, zeroing in on one person whom she can harass. She has her favorite victims, but we've all taken our turn in her cross-hairs. Whether it's a dress code violation or some other minor infraction, she finds some nitpicky thing to harp on.

To us, her presence is a mere irritation since she doesn't carry any real power. However, there are rumblings of a Chief Marketing Officer position opening in the Lincoln office that she has her eye on. She would be truly insufferable if that were to happen, but at least she'd be a hundred miles away. Over the years, we've come to realize she's all bark and no bite, but most newcomers cannot take constant criticism, and I was one of them. For some reason, the massive turnover rate at this location has not sent corporate enough red flags.

"Peters."

I hear her grating voice through my headphones, but I dare not turn around.

"Sandra, good morning!" Shelby practically chirps.

Her customer service voice comes naturally, but she jacks it up another notch with Sandra.

"I reviewed your marketing materials for the upcoming benefit, and all the header fonts are incorrect," she snaps, "I distinctly remember emailing you the new guidelines after our re-brand last quarter. That branding guide should be your Bible, sweetie."

"Right you are," Shelby says, unfazed, clicking away at her keyboard.

I throw a glance her way as she begins pulling up documents on her screen. "Here are the social ads you requested for the marketing campaign. And if you look right here, the font is Verdana Heavy, which *is* what is listed over here on the branding guide."

I dare not turn around, but I can tell by the silence that Sandra is taken aback.

"Well... it looks far too dark. We aren't going for this kind of look, you know," she says, voice dripping with disdain.

"Fix it, Peters," she says before stalking off like a wounded predator.

Once she's cleared the vicinity, I whistle low under my breath.

"Whew, that was smooth," I say in admiration. "This is why you're the queen!"

"You know what they say," she shoots me a wink, "You kill more flies with honey than vinegar."

"I'd prefer a flyswatter myself," Jenna laughs from the other side of the cubicle wall.

I chuckle and turn back to my desk. I pull a report from the latest email marketing campaign, creating a chart to showcase its performance. I see a sharp drop after the second week of the ad's run, and I drill down into the data to try to determine why.

It's well into the afternoon, and I still haven't found a root cause for this campaign tanking. I know Sandra and the other execs will have lots of questions come morning, but I have to get the rest of the report prepped and sent off.

Anxiety wraps around my belly as I gather my things to leave, but I try to push it out of my mind for now.

At home, I busy myself making supper. There is something

so peaceful in cooking that I nearly forget about everything else. It is freeing to ditch the recipe and add in a dash of this and a sprig of that. All the flavors combine in a new and different way, making the dish even more delicious than the last time it was made. Well… most of the time.

I wish life was like that, uncomplicated and without a set script I need to follow. My life has felt so stagnant lately. Maybe it's time to set the recipe aside and do what I want for a change. I need a greater purpose, but what?

Steam rises from the teal blue sauté pan, and the aroma of garlic and fresh rosemary wafts throughout the kitchen. Humming softly, I give the sauce one last stir before turning to the sink to drain the pasta. From the back door comes the clomp of heavy feet, and a moment later, Spencer appears.

"Hey baby," he says, dropping his oversized Igloo lunchbox on the counter. "Mmm, something smells good!"

"Rough day?" I ask, noticing the fresh grease stains on his hands and shirt.

"Jason's wife had her baby, so we're a man down this week," he says. "Then a conveyor broke down, and I helped the guys get it back up and running before my shift ended."

I clench my jaw and swallow the sudden knot in my throat. "You should wash up before dinner."

"Oh, should I?" he says with a mischievous glint sparkling in his eyes. "I figured I'd give my wife a big bear hug first!"

"Spencer, don't you dare!" I threaten, brandishing the wooden spoon. Unfazed, he begins stalking toward me with outstretched arms.

"Spencer! I'm wearing white!" I shriek as he edges closer, waggling his filthy fingers at me.

He flashes a wicked grin as I lurch away, only to find myself pressed against the kitchen sink.

"Gotcha!" he says, trapping me between his arms.

For a beat, our eyes lock, but I glance away and try to wiggle from his grasp. He gives me a gentle peck on the forehead before swiping one blackened finger across my nose as I break free.

"Ick! Was that really necessary?" I grumble, reaching for the dishrag and furiously scrubbing my face.

He chuckles softly and reaches behind me for the soap. While he cleans up, I assemble the salad and put the finishing touches on the pasta.

Crossing into the dining room, he pulls out my chair as I set down our plates. As he drops into his seat, he grabs the salt and pepper shakers and gives his entire plate of food a healthy coating.

"How do you know it needs that? You haven't even tasted it!"

"You know I always like a little extra salt," he says, shooting me a wink, "especially in my women!"

Annoyed, I roll my eyes, "Very funny."

Still feeling a bit miffed, I stare down at my plate and begin cutting my fettuccine into tiny pieces.

"Taylor, I'm only teasing. You know I love your cooking."

I nod slowly, still pouting internally, as he moves the conversation on.

"So, I've been thinking," he says. "I want to open my own welding business. I've been saving up my bonus checks, and I think if we're careful with spending, I can start buying some equipment. Maybe by the end of the year, I can look for a shop to rent."

"I don't know, Spence. You just got promoted to supervisor

last year. Do you really want to go back to the grind?"

"I just miss the work, you know?" he looks down, "Today is the first time I've gotten my hands dirty in a while. I don't want to be stuck in an office forever."

I chew slowly, processing this new information. I was so happy when he got his promotion last summer. It meant a permanent day shift, less backbreaking work, and the added bonus of a heftier paycheck.

He's finally elevated himself out of the blue-collar class and now wants to "get his hands dirty again." I just can't wrap my head around it.

"Owning your own shop is a lot different than just doing the work," I say, "There's so much you have to consider from a financial standpoint. Plus, there's still office work. You have books and accounts to manage, taxes…"

"I realize there's a lot to it…But I was thinking that's where we can work on this together."

Shit. He sees me as part of this venture? There are way too many things that could go wrong, and I can't let him down.

"There's just a lot to running a business." I say, trying to choose my words carefully, "I'm afraid you'd still run into the same issue of not being able to do the actual welding you enjoy."

All traces of the fun-loving Spencer is gone as he gives me a wounded look. "Is it that you don't think I'd *like* to run a business, or you don't think I *can*?"

For a moment, I don't know what to say. The question hangs in the air like smoke. Do I think he has the skill set to manage his own operation? Running a new business would also consume so much of his time, and I'm not sure I'm prepared for that. Plus, the startup cost alone requires capital that we don't have.

"Well?" He raises an eyebrow at me.

"I didn't say that," I murmur.

"Taylor, sometimes I feel-"

"Can we talk about this another time?" I cut him off.

Spencer grunts and stands abruptly. The chair leg squeaks against the hardwood floor as he pushes back from the table. Depositing his plate in the sink, he quietly sulks off to the living room.

I toy with the last few bites of pasta on my plate, mulling over the current situation. Spencer is rarely serious about anything. There is always a joke on the tip of his tongue and a boyish grin across his face. In a way, he's always been a big kid, which is both a blessing and a curse. Maybe working toward something that's *his* would be good for him.

He's the most selfless person I know, and he's everything to me. With every failed attempt at motherhood, Spencer helped pick up the pieces of my shattered heart. He has held my hand after every negative pregnancy test and brought me ice cream in the middle of the night when nightmares tore me from sleep.

He deserves this, but forever a pessimist, I only see all the ways this could drown us financially. And those alarm bells won't stop ringing. I do want him to be happy, and I can tell he hasn't been content in this new role. I've loved having him around more, but he isn't himself. He tries to hide it, but I see the weariness in his eyes that wasn't there before. Even when his body came home aching, he still had a sense of joy about him. I can tell that the spark is fading.

Deep down, I know I'm being selfish for tamping down his dream.

But why should he be able to have his dream when I can't?

Whoa, where'd that come from? That's a bit harsh even for me.

I cradle my head in my hands as my nightly headache settles in. I don't even know if his plan is feasible, so maybe I should just drop it for now.

Feeling settled at last, I rise from the table and set about my routine of tidying the kitchen. After giving the counters a thorough wipe-down, I turn to begin loading the dishwasher.

Ping!

I glance over to see that my phone is lit up. Lifting it from the cool laminate counter top, I see the reminder pop up: "APPT. Dr. Hatfield -Wednesday 9 a.m.!"

Instantly, my heart drops, and the plate in my other hand clatters into the sink basin. Suddenly, I no longer care about clean dishes. I snap the dishwasher door closed and trudge out of the room in desperate need of a hot shower and ibuprofen.

Chapter 3

On Wednesday, I show up for my appointment 10 minutes early, as always, and take the elevator to the 3rd floor. A soft ding sounds as the doors open, and I make my way down this dreaded hallway. My clammy feet slip inside my ballet flats. My palms are still stiff from clenching the steering wheel the entire drive across town. A mixture of fear and hunger has my stomach tied in knots as I take a seat after greeting the receptionist. She gives me a tight smile.

I've been here so many times that the staff knows me by name. I watch women in various stages of pregnancy come and go as if it's any other day of the week. Not for me. I'd rather be anywhere but here – somewhere I can pretend this isn't happening.

I watch the traffic on the highway three stories below me, watching the ant-like cars zipping off into the distance. How I wish I could flee the scene right along with them. But here I am waiting. Always waiting.

I pull out my phone and open my reading app, trying to

pull myself away from my reality into a fictional world. But I can't focus. I read the page again, but I'm too distracted by my nerves.

"Taylor?"

I lift my faux leather handbag off the chair beside me, shove my phone in the outside pocket, and follow my favorite nurse, Hallie, to the exam room. I comply with the typical procedure of weight, blood pressure, and the same line of questioning as every month.

I answer mechanically: The same old side effects. No LH surges. No basal body temperature spikes. Nothing. After stomaching that ordeal, I prepare myself to repeat it all back to Dr. Hatfield, who is going to ask me all the same questions anyway.

"Okay," Hallie says, snapping off her gloves, "Dr. Jensen will see you now."

"Wait," I say, confused, "Where's Dr. Hatfield?"

"Oh, he retired at the end of the year. Dr. Jensen is his replacement. You should have received a letter in the mail."

I nod and smile, taking in this information. Apprehension and relief fill me at the same time. I'm thankful that I will no longer have to endure Hatfield's constant criticism about my weight.

After a quick knock, a petite woman with long brown hair tied up in a jaunty ponytail steps into the room. A subtle blush highlights her lightly freckled cheeks, and her eyes look kind under dark, fringed lashes. If it weren't for her white coat and clipboard, I would have taken her for another nurse, and I chide myself internally for the assumption.

"Taylor Swanson?" she asks in an upbeat tone.

I give a brittle nod and prepare to recite my entire medical history.

"I see you've been trying to get pregnant for a few years." She says, not even glancing at the chart in her hand. "I took the liberty of studying your case before your appointment, and I think it's time to shake up your treatment."

I blink, a bit unsure what to say, and she continues.

"You've been on clomiphene for a while, huh? How's that been going?"

My words catch in my throat as I go over in my head the rollercoaster mood swings, piercing daily headaches, brutal hot flashes, and overall feeling of hopelessness.

"It doesn't seem to be doing anything for me," I say flatly.

"Yeah, it works great for some, and for others, not so much. You seem to be in the latter category," she says. She gives me a sympathetic look.

She leans back against the counter behind her and sets my chart down.

Two minutes into meeting her, and I feel like she's done more for me than Hatfield did in 5 years, and she hasn't done anything yet. She just listened to me.

"I have a game plan," she says, "you're going to have to bear with me."

She then proceeds to lay out the course of treatment for the next two months, including a double dose of clomiphene, monthly ultrasounds, and HCG shots.

"However," she cautions, "If we don't see results by March, it's time to explore other options."

I know this means expensive fertility specialists and procedures I can't possibly afford. Despite the looming deadline, I can't help but feel a touch of optimism. I finally have direction now, not just the same endless temperature tracking and medication over and over again. Lather, rinse, repeat.

"I'd also like to test your thyroid," she says, interrupting my thoughts. "A hormone imbalance can cause a lot of fertility issues."

I think back to my previous appointments with Dr. Hatfield and his constant fixation on my weight. One bad case of mono when I was 20 left me dangerously underweight, and that number has remained frozen in my chart ever since.

Despite several failed diet and exercise plans, I've never been able to get back to it, and Hatfield never failed to mention my BMI.

Chewing the corner of my lip, I gather the courage to speak, "You don't think this is weight-related?"

She gives me a funny look.

"I mean, regular exercise and a healthy diet are important for fertility, but I see nothing in your chart that concerns me in that area. Your weight is not a problem."

The corners of my lips turn up as I process her words. Maybe I'm not such a failure after all.

She asks if I have any other questions, and for the first time, I don't feel defeated at the end of an appointment. Dr. Jensen then reaches into the pocket of her lab coat to retrieve a business card and jots down a reminder to set up my next appointment and pick up my new prescription.

On her way out the door, she stops and briefly touches my shoulder.

With a warm smile, she says with confidence, "We're going to get you pregnant, girl."

There is a palpable shift in the air. Buoyed by her level of confidence, I make my way down the once-dreaded hallway and step into the elevator with a renewed sense of hope.

Smiling, I tap out a text to Spencer.

Good news! I have a new doctor and a new course of treatment. Maybe something is finally going to happen.

Chapter 4

A low beeping echoes through the dim room. In the air, the scent of hospital-grade disinfectants lingers. This once warm and cozy space no longer resembles my home. Gone are the matching Tiffany lamps on the nightstands, and in their place are strange medical machines and rows of amber-colored bottles.

Daddy looks at me with sadness, but he doesn't say a word. He simply wipes his face with his sleeve and steps away from the bed. Why won't he tell me what's happening?

I wrap my stiff fingers around the frail hand on the mattress, feeling the warmth there begin to fade. The steady rise and fall of her chest becomes shallower.

Panic sets in as the gravelly rasp in her lungs grows heavier and her breathing slows. A mumbled phrase escapes her pale lips as her sunken eyes meet mine one last time.

"Sweetheart," she says, excruciatingly slow, "Never forget who you are."

"I...love..." Her final words are cut short by a piercing scream from somewhere in the room.

Foreign arms wrap around my middle and pull me from her side.

What is happening? Who is grabbing me?

The edges of my vision darken as the room seems to fade away. I cry out for my mother one last time before everything goes black.

* * *

Gasping for air, I wake with a start. My palms are slick with sweat as my heart slams so hard against my ribcage I fear it will leave a bruise. I place my hand on my chest and try to ground myself. I'm in my bedroom. I'm safe.

My mother's death was nearly 2 decades ago, and yet the nightmare still plagues me. Kicking off the covers, I clamber out of bed and make my way across the hall to the bathroom. I splash some cold water on my face, trying to come back down to earth. I glance at my phone on its charger to see it's 2:15 a.m. Knowing it will be hours before I will be calm enough to sleep, I head toward the living room.

I glide my hand along the tall, built-in shelves Spencer designed when we first moved in. A few years later, he added a little reading nook in front of the tall bay windows. The cozy window seat has been my favorite spot in our house ever since.

I comb through the bookcase for some new reading and instead stop at the carved wood box on the top shelf. You could call it my "feeling sorry for myself box," because it's only opened when I'm feeling particularly gloomy.

Beneath the delicately carved lid reside three mementos that rarely see the light of day: a sterling silver cross pendant, a faded newspaper clipping, and a hand-knit pair of baby booties.

The latter was a wedding gift from my stepmother, Genie, "for your first baby to wear home from the hospital."

The words slice me open to this day.

I settle myself down in the window seat and reach for the nearby Tiffany lamp. With a flick of the switch, the reading nook is bathed in a low light.

I reach for a faded leather-bound journal, running my fingers over the cover. My father thrust it into my hands after a rather awkward family Christmas three years ago. He said he wanted me to have something of my mother's. The unexpected gift came on the heels of yet another negative pregnancy test, and at the time felt more like a poison than a present.

After that, I only came around for holidays, Leslie's school functions, or other family obligations. My dad and I haven't been able to carry on a conversation beyond the weather since I left.

I suppose after all these strained years, he meant the journal to be a peace offering of sorts, but it couldn't have come at a worse time, and I haven't seen him since. It was too painful to read my mother's words, and the journal got shoved in the back of my desk drawer for over a year.

I only recently rediscovered it while looking for the washing machine manual, but I have only been able to read a single entry at a time before I become overwhelmed by emotion.

She was such a lively woman, from her golden, unbound hair and brightly patterned dresses to the absolute joy she radiated into the world. I can hardly picture her settling down with my father.

Memories of her wash over me as I crack the cover and am greeted by her familiar, scripted handwriting.

July 4, 1994

Today, we brought home our new baby girl. There have been

so many laughs and tears shed these last few days. Taylor is an absolute blessing. I can hardly believe she's finally here!

I just want this sweet girl to stay perfect and tiny forever. My little ray of hope is currently sound asleep in her daddy's arms after the fireworks outside startled her awake.

Bradley is such an amazing father already. He just has this natural soothing way with her. Last night, she cried for 2 hours straight and only wanted him. I think I'm going to be sleep-deprived for the next year, but I am going to try to soak up every moment with her that I can.

I have been given a wonderful opportunity to be her mom, and I'll do everything in my power to keep her as happy and healthy as possible. I didn't know a person could love this much.

"As long as I'm living, my baby, you'll be."

My throat clogs as I read her description of my first night home from the hospital and the quote from my favorite bedtime story. I set the book aside and scrub my eyes with the palms of my hands. That's enough hurt for one night.

I reach for a worn copy of Pride and Prejudice instead, and before long, my eyelids grow heavy.

When I open my eyes, the hazy light of dawn is filtering through the gauzy curtain beside me. I'm still curled into the window seat, and as I come to life, I realize how stiff my body has become. I stretch my arms, trying to unwind the kinks in my muscles from sleeping in such an awkward position.

My legs protest as I rise to my feet and head toward the kitchen in search of coffee. I can already smell the scent in the air, which is odd, considering Spencer doesn't drink it.

"I don't know how you can drink that bitter stuff," he always says, "It's as dark as the devil himself."

He, of course, teases me for my love of a good, strong, dark roast. Don't give me that cream and sugar nonsense, I like my coffee plain Jane — just like me.

The smell of my favorite blend wafts toward me from the kitchen. Alongside the freshly brewed pot is a hastily scrawled note:

"Saw you fell asleep in your reading nook again. Figured you'd need this today. Love you. — S."

Glancing at the time on the stove, I see it is not even 6 in the morning. He must have left for work early again. We've barely seen each other for days now.

Things have been a bit chilly between us since our little tiff over his welding business. I've had the suspicion that he's avoiding me and, therefore, avoiding further conflict. That's the one thing about Spencer, he's a lover — not a fighter.

In many ways, he's far better than I deserve. This recent lull in our marriage is just more proof of that. I know I should be more supportive of him, but I get so wrapped up in my own baggage sometimes.

I pour myself a mug of coffee and sit down on a kitchen bar stool, contemplating life. If I didn't think to death everything in my life, I'd have so much more time to actually *do* things. There are times I wish I could find a way to claw myself out of my own mind long enough to enjoy the world around me.

I wish I could be more like Spencer — easy-going, never taking life too seriously. He doesn't need a plan for every minute of the day. He just takes everything in stride.

I shake my head and take another sip, letting the warmth fill me from the inside. I pull my phone out of my back pocket to send him a quick thank-you text for the coffee.

As I'm about to start typing, a notification pops up from my fertility tracking app.

Ovulation Day!

Terrific.

Chapter 5

I'm not sure what I was expecting last week when Dr. Jensen suggested adding the "trigger shot" to my treatment plan. Taking pills every month was more than enough for me. I despise needles, and the thought of one going near me gives me cold sweats. Spencer isn't much better. He wanted to come to the appointment today, but when I told him about the shot, his face visibly paled. I insisted I would be okay going by myself, although right now I might be regretting that.

I was certainly *not* expecting the shot to go in my hind end. On the positive side, not being able to see it go in was actually easier than any previous injections I've been forced into.

The other unexpected incident today was my ultrasound. I'm not sure how I've come this far in my infertility journey without one, a fact that also surprised my new doctor.

Paint me naive, but I was somehow completely unaware that most early ultrasounds are done… Well, let's just say *internally*.

Hollywood had convinced me that a little cold goo on your belly is the only inconvenience to this certain procedure. A magical wand slides around for a few seconds across your abdomen, and *Bibbidi Bobbidi Boo,* you have a perfect silhouette of a perfect baby.

Faced with my look of complete horror when asking me to undress from the waist down, the ultrasound tech calmly explained the process.

"I'm sorry, I didn't know..."

"It's okay, sweetie," she said patiently, "Most new patients are confused at first."

I gritted my teeth through the whole uncomfortable ordeal. This moment was not what I had ever pictured. Instead of gushing over fuzzy snapshots of a fetus, I got to get up close and personal with my ovaries.

"We're counting follicles," the tech had explained.

I nodded as if I perfectly understood, knowing full well I'd be Googling it the minute I left the building.

Now, sitting here on the exam table, I await Dr. Jensen's return. Paper crinkles under my butt as I shift uncomfortably. Surprisingly, the injection site isn't causing me undo irritation yet.

"Taylor," Dr. Jensen practically sings as she bursts into the room.

"Good news is that your thyroid test came back, and your levels are where they should be. Also, this last round of clomiphene seems to be working. It shows here that you have several follicles on your right side." She explains, "The trigger shot you received should signal your body that it is time to release the eggs. With any luck, there will be a positive pregnancy test in your near future."

"Wow," I say, slowly shaking my head.

Could it really be that simple? All these years of trying, and

I just needed a little shot in the ass?

Dr. Hatfield was so certain I was insulin resistant. He had me start tracking my basal body temperature, because in his words, "You can't trust those over-the-counter ovulation tests. The old-school method is best."

I took his word for it, and for three months, I faithfully tracked my temperature at the same time every morning on the photocopied line graph he sent home with me. In the end, it didn't tell me squat. Due to my inconsistent cycles, there was no detectable pattern, and the results were inconclusive.

When I followed up with him, he continued to push weight loss, insisting I must be insulin resistant and therefore not ovulating. But that test came back negative, too.

A year and a half passed before he finally suggested medication to induce ovulation, and clomiphene has been my nemesis ever since.

Dr. Jensen jots a note in my chart before handing me her card with a date scrawled on it.

"If you get a positive EPT, give me a call, and we'll set up your prenatal work. Otherwise, I'll put in that new prescription, and I'll see you back here on day 12 of your next cycle for another scan."

I take the card out to the nurse's station to schedule next month's ultrasound appointment. So many thoughts are swirling in my head. Is this finally going to happen for me?

I try to clear my head by listening to my favorite audiobook version of *Pride and Prejudice*, as I drive from the clinic to my office.

I step through the sliding glass doors, still daydreaming about Mr. Darcy. Coming in two hours later than usual is going to land me on Sandra's radar. Since the latest marketing report dropped, she's zeroed in on me. Firing off dozens of questions about the mysterious dip in the campaign numbers — questions I haven't had answers to.

I quickly cross the room and plop into my chair next to Shelby.

"Sandra in today?" I ask in a low voice.

"Nope. Called out sick."

I shouldn't wish illness on anyone, but I'm okay with having some breathing room today. If I could just take a deeper look at those numbers…

"How'd the lady doc go?" Shelby spins to face me. "You good on paps for the next three years?"

"Uh, yeah, I guess," I say dumbly and power up my computer.

I'm not sure why I haven't confided in my best friend about my fertility struggles. Her resistance to any sort of domestic life makes me feel like she wouldn't understand. She would never trade in her career and freedom for a husband and kids, and I love her for that. But she'll also never know the devastation I feel with every negative pregnancy test.

After getting caught up with my inbox and drafting a customer churn report I've been putting off, the rest of the day passes in a haze.

On the way home, I swing by the store for a few items on my grocery list. A tune plays on repeat in my head, although I can't quite bring the words to mind. I stifle the urge to hum out loud as I scour the grocery store aisle.

I've been meaning to locate a certain local barbecue sauce that Spencer absolutely loves. But given that it has become wildly popular, it is impossible to find. I'm hoping that today, I will be in luck.

A few paces ahead of me on the top shelf, my eyes notice

something shiny. The fluorescent lighting glints off the infamous golden bottle. An older store worker stocking ketchup nearby is blocking my access to it. However, it appears that he's nearly finished, so I hang back, feigning interest in the generic brands before me.

At that moment, a middle-aged woman with graying hair and an overloaded cart zips around me. She darts in front of the worker, snatches the coveted bottle, and quickly wheels her cart away.

Defeat crashes over me as I blow out an exasperated breath. I drop the bottle of store-brand sauce I had been studying into my basket and trudge away.

So much for surprising Spencer. I hang my head, wishing I could just be more confident. But here I am, as timid as a church mouse who would rather drop dead than inconvenience someone.

The same unknown melody and a handful of unhappy thoughts invade my mind as I drive home with my barbecue sauce riding shotgun.

Later in the kitchen, I set about preparing a marinade for the pork chops. I dump some of the sauce into a bowl and take a cautious sniff. It's not bad. It's not good either.

I dash around the kitchen, collecting ingredients and dumping things together. Splash of mango hot sauce. Cup of brown sugar. Squeeze of maple syrup. Spoonful of apple cider vinegar. Pinch of salt.

I take a bit of the concoction on a spoon and taste. Better, but not gourmet. Glancing at the clock, I realize I've spent too much time doctoring this up and need to start the chops cooking.

Without thinking, I grab the bottle of liquid smoke, pour a

generous amount in, and head outside to light the grill.

I'm just finishing up the salad, admiring the grill marks on the still-steamy chops, as I hear Spencer come in.

"Oo, baby," He bellows in an exaggerated Southern drawl, "Something smells spicy!"

He takes a deep breath over the plate of meat and moans.

"I do love your cooking," he states, leaning in for a peck on the cheek.

I roll my eyes, knowing full well that my rendition of barbecue is nothing compared to his. He takes grilling and smoking to a whole other level. Having won several barbecue competitions over the years, the man knows his way around a grill.

We sit down to eat, and I find myself glancing at him, trying to gauge his reaction to the plate before him. I feel myself holding my breath as he brings the first forkful to his lips.

"Mmmm, Baby!" he exclaims. "How did you manage to track down the gold label Sam's Secret Sauce? That stuff is harder to find than a gold nugget in the Sandhills!"

"The store was sold out of it," I mumble a half-truth. "This is generic. I just threw some things in to jazz it up."

"Hmm…" He dips his index finger into the sauce and brings it up to his lips. "You're right, it's not quite the same."

His brow furrows as if he's analyzing every nuanced flavor. He smacks his lips a couple of times, still concentrating.

"Little twang of mango, a bit of heat, and a smoky aftertaste," he mumbles to himself like some sort of high-end food critic.

"Okay, Gordon Ramsay," I tease him.

Ignoring my comment, he finally meets my eye, "This might be even better than Sam's. Definitely keep this recipe!"

I chuckle softly to myself, and he gives me a questioning

look.

"I pulled a Spencer and just dumped crap together. I have no idea what's in here."

"I've always said measurements are overrated." He laughs, "Except in this case. We have to re-create this sauce!"

The dark mood that's been hanging over us for weeks seems to lift like fog in the sunlight. For the rest of the meal, the conversation flows easily between us. Just the way it used to.

"So…" I begin hesitantly. "Dr. Jensen thinks the meds are working. I'm actually ovulating."

"Baby," he breathes, "That's amazing. Maybe this is finally going to happen for us." He reaches for my hand and tenderly kisses my fingers.

I smile softly before standing to clear the table. As I head for the sink, I find myself humming the same tune that has been pestering me all day. Water fills the basin as I rinse the saucepan and salad bowl before loading everything into the dishwasher.

Suddenly, there is harmony in the room, and I realize that Spencer has joined in. The familiar song lingers in my memory. I swear I've heard it a thousand times, but where?

At last, the memories and the words come flooding back.

"Do you remember spinning around on that dance floor?" he whispers in my ear.

I nod, recalling the pinch of my too-tight heels and swish of ivory taffeta as we exchanged our wedding vows.

He lowers his lips to mine for the first time in what feels like forever. Abandoning the sauce-stained dinnerware to soak in the sink, he leads me down the hallway.

In the bedroom, his hands deftly work the buttons of my blouse until the material falls away from my body. Hot kisses trace up the side of my neck while I struggle to fill my lungs with air.

I hold onto him like he's the only thing left in my world. His mouth crashes down on mine once more, and we tumble onto the bed. My skin is scorched from his touch as our bodies collide together in the sweetest way possible.

Suddenly, he pulls back and looks into my eyes. Like a vow, he whispers against my lips the lyrics to "I Swear" that I'd nearly forgotten.

John Michael Montgomery's ballad lingers in my mind as we drift to sleep, tangled in each other's arms.

* * *

I wake in the night to a rolling sensation in my gut. Not feeling the energy to drag myself out of bed, I reach for the lukewarm bottle of water on the nightstand.

I grimace at the metallic taste of the water as my stomach lurches again. I run my hands over my face and roll to my side, burrowing back into the warmth of the covers.

I reach my hand out and place it on the warmth of Spencer's back. I find myself grounded by the feeling of his heartbeat beneath my fingers, muscles contracting as he breathes in and out. Oftentimes, this simple touch reassures me when I find myself awake in the middle of the night. It is reassuring to know that this man chose me when I've so often felt unworthy of love.

In these moments, I realize I can't live without him. This man, this skin and flesh and bones, they are precious to me. I would rather bicker with him over how to file taxes than lie beside anyone else. He deserves someone better than me —

someone who can finally give him his dream.

I swallow my guilt and settle back against his side. He's still fast asleep, and before long, I feel myself fading as well.

As the early light of dawn slants through the bedroom window, I pull myself out of bed. The nausea from the night before has dissipated, so I decide to whip up some breakfast.

In the kitchen, I begin to pull out the ceramic flour and sugar canisters. I frown at a box of pancake mix in the cupboard. Spencer swears the boxed stuff tastes better, but I think it's just an excuse not to make the real deal.

Within minutes, I'm whisking the batter in a large bowl as steam rises from the nearby griddle.

There's something special about Sunday mornings in the winter. There is still a chill lingering in the house as the golden sunlight reflects off the lingering snow outside.

I find myself continuing to hum our wedding song as I carry a platter of sweet-smelling confection and a mug of hot cocoa to the bedroom.

Spencer is still softly snoring as I waft the scent of maple and vanilla pancakes toward his nose. At once, his eyes snap open as he pulls himself up in bed.

"Oh man, these smell great, baby!" His eyes shine with delight.

The image comes to mind of a cartoon hobo drooling over a pie on a windowsill, and I stifle a giggle.

He sets the plate aside and instead reaches for me, pulling me down across his lap playfully. The suppressed laugh escapes me as his arms encircle my back. He tucks a strand of hair behind my ear and places a gentle kiss on my forehead. That simple gesture reignites last night's flame.

But this time it's different. His lips are gentle and soft as they angle over mine. My hands slide up the rippling muscles of his biceps and cup the sides of his face. The two-day-old stubble on his cheeks scratches my palms as I pull myself in deeper. His work-worn hand caresses the back of my neck, and his fingers delve into my hair.

Loving the feeling of his fingers twining through the strands along my scalp, I let out a soft moan. Encouraged, he begins toying with the hem of my T-shirt. His featherlight touch sends shivers up my spine as he traces circular patterns on my skin.

Like the night before, we become lost in the moment and in each other. With breakfast long forgotten, our bodies come together in a sensuous dance of limbs and warm skin.

Spent and satisfied, I collapse on my side of the bed. My heavily lidded eyes gaze up at him as I bask in the afterglow. I trace the hard lines of muscle along his abdomen as he reaches across me for the breakfast platter.

"There's nothing wrong with cold pancakes," Spencer grins and winks at me.

"Pfft!" I scoff and roll my eyes at him, but for some reason, I can't keep this grin off my face.

He makes a face as he sips from the cooling mug of cocoa.

"I can't do cold hot chocolate, though," he says, hauling himself up off the bed.

He heads for the door in only his boxer shorts, "Be right back, I'm going to go nuke this."

Taking a bite from the nearest maple-drenched pancake, I realize he's actually right — they are still pretty good. I place my hand against my stomach as a feeling of unease grips me again. Maybe I'll just stick with coffee this morning.

Chapter 6

Over the next two weeks, my relationship with Spencer seems lighter than it has been in years.

It's bitter cold and a Monday at that, but I'm still soaring on a metaphorical cloud nine. I'm not even sure what possessed someone to count clouds in the first place. I make a mental note to Google it during my lunch break.

"Good morning, gorgeous!" I greet Shelby as I enter our cubicle space.

"Damn, you're cheery this morning!" she states, "What's the occasion, did the Packers win last night?"

I roll my eyes, "No, Shelby. They lost in the playoffs."

"Whatever," she snarks, "You know I can't keep track of all this sports nonsense. I mean, big buff guys are great to look at and all, but no one pays attention to the actual game!"

I chuckle, ignoring her jab about my football fandom, "No, I'm just in a good mood today. What's wrong with that?"

"It's just suspicious," she narrows her eyes at me, "I feel like something catastrophic is going to happen."

I make a face at her. "Don't be dramatic. Can't a woman just be happy?"

"You know I love you, Tay-tay…" she starts.

"Ugh!" I interrupt her, "Really Tay-Tay, again?"

"As I was saying," she continues, "This is a change of pace. Happiness looks good on you."

"You say that as if I'm moody and depressive all the time."

"Don't take this the wrong way. . . But I don't know, you just have a dark aura about you most of the time."

She makes a fluttery motion with her hands as if I'm emitting some sort of bad juju into the universe.

I raise an eyebrow at her, but internally, I chew on her words. She has a point. I've never been a particularly *exuberant* person, but I didn't realize that my sarcasm came off in such a dark way.

I put the thoughts aside as I pull up Excel and begin entering figures for this week's sales report that I've been drowning in. My brain gets drawn into the numbers as it always does. I don't happen to glance up until it's nearly lunch time and I realize I'm absolutely starved.

I spin around in my chair just as Shelby is collecting her coat and purse. Jenna approaches our cubicle already bundled up for the frigid winter weather. The two begin to banter about the daily lunch special at the café down the street.

"You guys headed out for a bite?" I pipe up from my desk.

"Yeah, Freddy's will be packed if we don't get a move on," Jenna says with a touch of annoyance in her tone.

"I'm coming, I'm coming," Shelby mutters, zipping up her puffy winter coat.

"You guys have room for one more?" I blurt.

Shelby stops mid-zip and stares at me.

"We invite you all the time, but you never come out with us."

"I dunno.." I shrug my shoulders, not sure myself what prompted me to ask.

"Sure! The more, the merrier," Jenna says, "Let's just get a move on. I'm getting hangry."

I stay mostly silent as our trio rushes down the street. Luckily for Jen, there are only a few people in line, so we are seated quickly.

Within minutes, three glasses of water with lemon and three coffees are plopped down in front of us. I instantly reach out to warm my frozen fingers on the steaming mug and breathe in the glorious scent.

As our food arrives, pressed sandwiches and hand-cut fries, the conversation shifts from idle office chit-chat and somehow centers on me.

"You seem different," Jen says, nibbling on a corner of her BLT.

"She definitely does. I said as much this morning," Shelby points a fry accusingly in my direction.

"Maybe she's finally getting laid?"

Snickers erupt on their side of the booth as I blush furiously.

"Guys, I'm right here," I say defensively.

"Don't get all huffy," Shelby says, "It's a good thing. You're not wound up tighter than a tick for once."

I cock an eyebrow at her.

"Yeah, you almost have a light about you," Jenna says dramatically, "Like a *lit from within* glow. If you found a new highlighter, you have to spill!"

"Yeah. Don't gatekeep makeup. These are must-know matters."

I roll my eyes.

"I just remembered why I don't go out with you two."

I smirk at them, only half joking. Cause, dang. They sure know how to put a person in the hot seat. But something Jenna says sticks in my mind. Glow?

I stay quiet through the remainder of our meal as their chit-chat moves on to their love life woes. I barely listen as they swap stories of first dates and romances gone horribly wrong.

My recent bouts of nausea flash before me, and I start counting the days in my head. My foot taps anxiously under the table.

With food polished off and checks paid, we gather our items and head out into the snow.

"I'm going to run an errand quick. I'll see you back in the office," I say abruptly, turning down a side street.

The two look a bit startled as I hurry away in the cold.

Maybe it is the bitter Midwest wind or possibly my jangled nerves. But something has my fingers trembling as I tear open the cellophane wrapper. Hunched over in a drug store bathroom is not how I imagined my lunch break today. Although I could have waited until I got home, the *need-to-know* urge was stronger than my patience.

I've taken dozens of these tests over the years, but somehow this feels different. I feel it in my gut, or maybe in my womb? This time, that second line is going to show up. I know it. I start the timer on my watch.

Why does three minutes feel like an eternity? My entire life is about to change, and it's mere seconds away. I watch the countdown timer on my phone. The pregnancy test is face down in my hands. I'm too scared to look. I don't want to ruin it by looking at it before the time is up. Which I realize is a ridiculous notion.

My head is reeling, and I realize I'm slowly rocking back and forth.

If someone were to burst this stall door open, they'd likely mistake me for an addict or a madwoman. Pants around my ankles, body shaking, and clutching a piece of plastic with a death grip. I'm sure I look completely unhinged.

"Faith," I whisper under my breath. "I know you're there. Please be there."

I press my hand to my belly, trying to will a baby into existence. The sweet baby girl I've been dreaming about for years. The one I've already named and imagined an entire life for. She has sweet, rosy cheeks and soft, downy hair. She's perfect. My Faith Marie. I know she's finally here.

The ticking stopwatch catches my eye: 3,2,1.

I take a deep breath in through my nose and slowly release it. My eyes squeeze shut as I slowly flip the stick over. Holding it in my still-trembling hand, I slowly crack my eyelids and stare at the display.

Negative.

I shatter instantly.

Chapter 7

I turn the page on my desk calendar and scowl. The first of the month always means a flurry of activity in the office. Beth, the accounting clerk, is in a frenzy getting invoices out the door for customers and reconciling the January books. Jenna has been on the phone all day conducting monthly client surveys, and I am vehemently putting off the marketing report that needs to be finalized before tomorrow's February strategy meeting. The columns on my spreadsheet are blurring together, and I can't seem to focus.

Shelby, who is mysteriously absent today, has once again found marketing gold with her latest campaign. Her conversion numbers are always phenomenal compared to some of the other marketers, which is part of the reason Sandra typically steers her venom elsewhere. Jenna is an up-and-comer, but she has a way to go before she surpasses Shelby. Spending a few years in this business has helped Shelby have a leg up on some of the "fresh blood" that comes straight off the bus from the local university with a bright, shiny Business Marketing degree.

Shelby has been in the trenches long enough to know what actually works, not just some memorized textbook strategies. I crunch her numbers and analyze website traffic to see which tactics hit and which ones miss.

There's a constant rivalry between marketers to see who has the best campaign for the month, whose ad gets the highest number of eyeballs, and who has the highest conversion rate. Why we can't all work together as a team is beside me. Corporate seems to think pitting us all against each other will increase productivity and make us fight tooth and nail to get ahead. But in actuality, it causes the best to jump ship while the lazy and lifeless continue to linger.

Shelby and I are tenured enough that it's impossible to leave, and instead, we watch the endless lifecycle of good employees burning out only to be replaced by younger, less motivated college grads who leave at the first hint of trouble.

There used to be five data analysts, each working with our five marketers. Now we're short a few bodies, and I've taken on the brunt of the workload. I'm pulling numbers for three different campaigns and have reports to compile on a daily and weekly basis. Quite frankly, I'm drowning.

I dig my fingers into the corners of my eyes, hoping to remedy the dizzying effect of the spreadsheet and the glare of my monitor. I can already feel a headache coming on like a thunderstorm brewing.

I hear the office hubbub around me as phones ring, nearby salespeople chatter to prospective clients, and computer mice click. The sound seems to rise in intensity. Everything and everyone is in motion — except me. I'm stuck in this quicksand of a life, going nowhere and about to be pulled under the surface.

My lungs feel squeezed, and I find myself fighting for breath. My head drops to my hands, and I try to claw my way back to some semblance of sanity.

"Taylor, I need to talk to you!"

I swivel in my seat on high alert at the tone of Shelby's voice as she rushes into our cubicle. That concern doubles when I see a look of sheer panic on her face.

"Shelby?" I say, rising from my chair and grasping her forearm. "Is everything okay?"

Wordlessly, she grabs my wrist and tugs me along after her. She practically drags me down the hall to the women's restroom. After doing a quick check of each stall for the feet of unwanted listeners, she whips around to face me.

"I'm pregnant."

I feel like the wind has been knocked out of my lungs, and the pain lances my chest like a knife to the gut. The words seem to hang in the air as a pressure builds behind my eyes, but I refuse to shed a tear.

"What?" I finally manage to get out.

"I'm pregnant, Taylor." She says with tears welling in her eyes, "I'm pregnant, and I don't know what to do."

She begins frantically pacing back and forth in the small room as if she's about to come unglued. Stuttering and stumbling, she blurts out her story.

"I-I was with this guy from the club last month, and I don't know. He must not have been careful. I was a couple days late, and-and I took a test the other day after our lunch."

That fact has my wicked heart sinking even lower. The same day, I took that damned test in a drug store bathroom. I paste a sympathetic look on my face and nod, prompting her to continue.

"Oh, Taylor," she says, turning toward me, "What am I going to do? I don't know the first thing about being a mom!"

"Why are you asking me?" I say, trying to keep the bite out of my tone.

"You're the most responsible person I know. You always know what to do. You're practically a mom to me."

She says that last bit with a half-smile. I know she means well, but she has no idea how deeply those words have sliced me open. I press my lips together hard to keep the emotions tamped down while scrambling for the right words to say.

"You know you have options . . ." I trail off awkwardly because I can't even bear the thought.

I would give anything in this world for a baby, and I can't fathom anyone making that choice.

"I know, I know," she mutters, looking down, "I just don't think I can give this up either."

Her hand gently rests on her lower abdomen as she speaks, and a shot of jealousy surges through me. My cheeks heat as an unexpected rage begins to rise within me. I mentally brace myself as I slowly step forward to embrace her. She sobs silently against my shoulder as I try to comfort her.

"It's okay, Shelb," I say soothingly, "We'll figure this out, you're not alone."

Meanwhile, I feel like I've been dropped into a 50-foot pit on a deserted island. I try to calm my breathing.

Pulling back and wiping her eyes, she smiles shyly, "Thanks, Taylor, you're the best friend I've ever had."

Her words tug at my heart for a moment. I doubt she'd say that if she knew my envious thoughts. I give her a tight smile and motion for us to leave the bathroom. I wish I could be happy for her, but inside, I'm so angry. How could this happen to someone so reckless when I have been trying for so long?

My phone buzzes as we make our way back to the cubicle.

"Hey sis, I've been trying to call you. We NEED to get together to talk wedding plans!!"

* * *

The last thing I want to be doing right now is discussing color schemes and caterers. I have been avoiding Leslie for this very reason. I love my baby sister. I do. But this is just too much.

She's been planning her wedding day since she was 7 years old. I don't understand how there are still *so* many decisions to make. Roses or carnations for the bouquet? How much lace is too much for the bridesmaid dresses? Candles or antique silver frames for the centerpieces? Or both?

I remember my simple backyard ceremony with my thrifted dress and a handful of close friends and family. We didn't bother with all these details. I was in such a hurry to get on with the rest of our lives. Now I'm not sure what for. Not much has happened on this side of tying the knot.

I envy my sister's naivety. This wedding may come straight from a princess movie, but the lifetime that follows will turn mundane quickly. Or heartbreaking.

They say that jealousy is the thief of happiness, and comparing yourself to others robs you of your individuality. But there are a lot of things that "they say."

Everywhere I turn, I am constantly reminded of all the things I *should* be grateful for. Yes, I know, life can always be worse. But damn. Life could also be a whole lot better.

I never told Spencer about the negative pregnancy test last

week, but I think he could feel the shift in my mood. My period came the next day, and with it came the reminder that motherhood is not in the cards for me yet again. Since then, I've endured the same mind-numbing headaches and crushing depression that come with every dose of clomiphene. Those symptoms are currently making this outing excruciating.

While I pull up to the quaint little bridal boutique, my mind goes to a dark place. Why do good things happen to undeserving people? I realize it is a terrible thing to think, but I can't let it go. This is my double-edged sword: Seething with envy while knowing how dangerous it can be.

I hate watching someone else go through everything I wish I could have. I long for that positive pregnancy test. The day we decorate the nursery and bring that baby home. Watching that baby learn to walk, and talk, and do long division.

But it has become a quickly fading dream that will never see reality. The name I picked out sits unused on the shelf of my mind, never meant to be. There will never be another Faith Marie Swanson.

In a few days, I'll get my final trigger shot and with it my last chance at being a mom. Without very painful and very expensive fertility treatments, I won't ever have the chance to have my own child. I just wanted a piece of my own mother with me — a little girl with her golden hair and joyful smile.

I take a deep breath. Today can't be about me. Despite the war raging in my mind, I need to be present for Leslie. Exhaling, I try to push the clouds out of my mind as I enter the shop.

My sister is dressed in white slacks with a floral blouse and a pastel pink blazer. The rock on her finger looks even bigger in person as she rushes forward to greet me with a giddy smile and flailing arms.

"Yay! You're here," she says, pulling me in for a quick hug, "I can't wait to get started!"

True to her personality, she's already picked out about a dozen dresses to try on. She hurries off with the salesgirl to the dressing room, and I gaze out over the sea of white dresses lining the racks of the store. This is *absolutely* not my scene.

I'm so zoned out, I don't even notice Leslie coming in from the fitting room and preening in front of the full-length mirror. It's not until I hear her voice that I turn back around.

"Ugh, this looked better on the hanger," she says, disappointedly shuffling back toward the fitting room.

A moment later, I hear a muffled cry from behind the drawn curtain.

"Um... I think I need help."

With the salesgirl helping another guest at the front counter, I step into the fitting room to find her flouncing helplessly, trapped within a mountain of tulle. Always the faithful sister, I move to unzip the fluffy behemoth so she can breathe again.

Leslie's cheeks flame, and there's an odd gleam in her eyes. For a moment, it looks like she's about to tear up. Like she's an actual human with real insecurities instead of a Barbie come to life. Empathy washes over me as I take the dress from her and drape it back over the hanger.

"That was supposed to be a size 2." I tell her. "I think it's mislabeled."

"You're probably right." She gives me an appreciative smile, brushing off any lingering embarrassment. "Besides, it was too late 90's for my taste. I'm wanting a more sleek and modern look."

She rattles on about mermaid skirts and necklines, completely oblivious to my mental turmoil. I must have a fairly decent poker face.

I spend the next hour dutifully playing my part, helping her in and out of at least a dozen dresses. I watch as she struts back and forth in front of the mirror, analyzing her reflection from every angle. When asked, I provide some vague response that reaffirms whatever opinion she's already made on said dress.

The endless parade of white and the glare of the overhead lights is making my head throb. Frankly, this whole process is exhausting for me, but Leslie thrives in this environment. With her looks and personality, she could walk the runway for a living instead of teaching second grade.

I idly drum my fingers on the padded seat beside me while Leslie changes into yet another gown. Glancing up, I see my sister emerging from the curtained dressing room.

Climbing the pedestal to get a better view of it, she suddenly becomes eerily quiet. With a modest sweetheart neckline and A-line skirt, the satin material clings to her in all the right places. The lace appliques across the bodice bring a touch of charm to the otherwise simple but elegant design.

Suddenly, I'm painfully aware that Leslie is the spitting image of our mother. In fact, Mom's dress was not so different from the one Leslie wears now. I remember the photo of my parents' wedding in the gilded frame that still sits on the mantel of my childhood home. The vintage gown had a bit more lace, and the original color was obscured by sepia tones, but Mom and Leslie could be twins.

My heart aches at the thought, and yet another green-eyed monster emerges from the swamp of my mind. I swallow a lump in my throat as I hear Leslie sniffle.

I glance up to see her carefully dabbing at the corners of her eyes with a tissue, keeping her makeup perfectly intact.

"Are you okay?" I ask, stepping forward.

"I just wish Mom could see this."

I visibly flinch. Leslie was in kindergarten when Mom was diagnosed with cancer, and I'd be willing to bet she has few memories of her that don't include a hospital bed. In some ways, I still resent the fact that my father could move on and have a whole new life. After Mom passed, there was no mention of her, no fond memories shared. He just shut down. Then suddenly, Genie was in the picture, and Mom was long forgotten. It didn't help that I never had much of an opportunity to know my stepmother. Shortly after their wedding, I graduated, married Spencer, and moved an hour away from my grief.

Leslie steps back down from the pedestal, and her damp eyes meet mine for the first time all afternoon.

"You don't know what it means to me that you're here," her voice quavers as she pulls me into her arms.

The unexpected display of emotion from my typically upbeat sibling has thrown me off. For the second time in less than a week, I find myself in the too-tight embrace of a teary-eyed female.

Unsure what to do, I pat her back awkwardly a few times before she eventually pulls back. I don't think we've hugged since we were instructed to do so after one of our many squabbles as children.

The compounded guilt I feel over my twisted feelings of envy ties my stomach in knots.

"I love you, Taylor," she says with sincerity.

I smile numbly as the peal of laughter from a nearby bride-to-be snaps us out of our moment.

Releasing a deep sigh, the sadness on her face clears.

"Now help me out of this, will you? I need to find the salesgirl. This is definitely the one!"

While working the zipper, I catch a glimpse of the price tag and internally cringe. The things I could do with $2,500. Nearly the cost of a consultation with a fertility specialist.

No.

I'm tamping those thoughts down. For now.

Chapter 8

How ridiculously ironic to be ovulating on Valentine's Day. As if I didn't already hate this holiday.

So far, my day has been great — one jab in the butt of HCG and a scathing lecture from Sandra about taking time off work without a one-week notice. Like I can tell my stubborn reproductive system to ovulate when it is more convenient for her.

Spencer texted after my appointment with Dr. Jensen that he had made reservations for tonight at a new steakhouse downtown. I think he's trying to ease the mounting tension of what tonight will bring.

Our last shot at parenthood.

I swallow hard and try to stay focused on the strategy meeting, but my mind is elsewhere. What if it doesn't take this time? How will we ever afford IVF? Could I even handle being impaled by a 17-gauge needle?

My stomach clenches at that. The trigger shots and blood draws I've endured are bad enough. I can't even think about egg retrieval without getting nauseous.

I keep my head down as Sandra drones on about keeping personal items on our desks to a minimum and limiting office chatter.

"I should only be hearing your voices when you're on the phone with clients," she says in the general direction of the sales team.

I glance at Shelby and roll my eyes, and she smirks back at me. She narrows her eyes in a classic Sandra sneer, and I chuckle under my breath.

"Swanson?" Sandra's shrill voice calls across the room. "Is there something funny back there?"

My cheeks flame as every head in the room swivels in my direction. I lower my gaze to the floor.

"Nope. I just thought of something funny," I say, shaking my head.

She frowns. "Next time, keep the comedy at home."

Shelby mouths an apology at me, and I shrug it off. This day sucks.

After my humiliation, the meeting adjourns, and everyone begins filing out. I finish up a few last-minute things, clean off my desk (you're welcome, Sandra), and shut down my computer.

At home, I'm running a few minutes behind, so I rush to get ready. I swap out my black slacks and polo for a flowy tan blouse, dark blue jeans, and low-heeled boots. I add a few swipes of mascara to my eyelashes and don some faux pearl earrings.

I'm just spritzing on some perfume when Spencer comes home covered in grease.

"Sorry, I'm late, babe." He says, seeing my confusion, "We were a man down on the line today, so I pitched it. Give me a second to shower, and we'll get going."

I let out a sigh as I glance at my watch. If the reservation is at 6:00, we'll barely make it there on time. I tap my foot impatiently as he lumbers to the bathroom to get cleaned up.

Ten minutes later, he emerges in a western shirt and faded jeans with wet, tousled hair. I swear he takes forever pulling on his cowboy boots.

"Are you ready?" I say a bit too impatiently.

Unbothered by my snark, he gets up in search of his wallet and keys.

"At this rate, we're not even going to make it in time for dessert," I mumble under my breath.

"What's that?" Spencer asks with one hand on the door.

"Nothing."

I brush past him and hurry to the car. We don't talk the whole drive. The nearest parking spot is two blocks from the restaurant, and by the time we get inside, it's 6:15.

Despite his boyish charm, Spencer is unsuccessful in convincing our hostess to honor our reservation, and we're turned away instead.

Outside, I take off walking toward the car at a fast clip with Spencer trailing behind. It has started to flurry, and the wind rips at my face. It might as well tear the rest of me away, too. I don't feel like there's much left.

A bitter feeling boils in my gut. If Spencer wasn't so damn preoccupied with "getting his hands dirty," he would have been home on time, and we would have made our reservation. I know I'm being unfair but tonight was supposed to be special.

We should be in there now with a glass of Moscato and a bottle of Coors, making eyes over our appetizers. I'd be feeling fizzy and lighthearted as we talked about our future together.

Now I'm out here doing cardio to escape the fucking cold. Arriving at the car, I wait while Spence fumbles with the keys to unlock the door. With each second, my temper swells.

Finally, the car honks and the locks click. I fling open the car door, jump inside, and slam it shut. Spencer starts the car and cranks up the heater. For a minute, no one says a word.

"I really am sorry, Taylor."

I nod but remain silent. I know I'm not being entirely reasonable. Maybe it was selfish to want a bit of romance. I've been in a crap mood for weeks, and I was hoping tonight I could just forget everything. Now what? We get takeout, go home, and have emotionless sex just to check a box, because it's our last chance, and we have to?

"Hey," he says, gently squeezing my hand, "why don't we try to salvage the rest of our night?"

"Yeah, okay." I say half-heartedly.

I squash down my negativity for the moment as he drives to our second favorite steakhouse. We wait forever to be seated, the food comes out cold, and by the end of it, I'm ready for bed. But at home, we still have one last task to complete.

Afterward, Spencer rolls over and falls promptly to sleep as I lie awake and stare at the ceiling. A lone tear of self-pity drops down my cheek and runs into my ear. This is not how tonight was supposed to go.

* * *

"Why are these open rates dropping so much?" I mutter under my breath.

Clicking into the details, I notice an uptick in unsubscribes and spam complaints in our latest email campaign. Something is wrong. I send off a quick email to Sandra detailing my findings and hope it's not too late to course correct.

"God, I feel like shit," Shelby moans next to me.

She's been whining nonstop about her morning sickness today, and frankly, it's making me queasy. But that could just be jealousy digging and twisting my insides.

"Don't they make like supplements or something you can take?"

"My doctor recommends ginger tea, but it's fucking gross."

"I'm sorry, dude. That sucks."

I'm not really sure what else to say. Part of me wants to scream at her to stop being so selfish. I'd happily take her place and deal with a little bit of nausea. But I bite my tongue. For better or worse, Shelby is my best friend. She'd probably be more sensitive if she knew about my predicament, but it somehow feels wrong to tell her now.

"I need a distraction," she says, lifting her head from her desk. "How are things with Spencer?"

I think back to the shitshow of a Valentine's date and the two weeks of stilted silence that followed.

"I don't know," I say, shrugging noncommittally, "They're fine, I guess."

"Come on," Shelby whines, "I need some big juicy details. As you can assume, my love life has officially ground to a halt. I need to live vicariously through you now."

I roll my eyes. When did the tables turn?

"Dude, we're married. We go home each night to a plain spaghetti dinner, watch Wheel of Fortune, and go to bed. There's not much to tell."

Shelby scoffs, but I notice a tinge of sadness in her eyes. "Whatever. If I can't live vicariously through your love life, why don't you at least go enjoy sushi and deli meat on my behalf?"

That I can do. As Shelby moseys off to the bathroom, I make a mental note to pick up a few rolls from the Japanese place downtown on my way home.

I skim through a few texts from Leslie about potential bridesmaid dresses. I veto one with a plunging neckline and thigh-high slit. I am far too old to be parading around with that much skin showing. She wants a sage and lavender color palette, and I have a love-hate relationship with it. I can't stand lavender. The flower. The scent. The color. And I am definitely not okay with poofy lavender bridesmaid dresses. I've hated them since I was 17, when I had to wear one in my father's wedding to Genie.

I text her my thoughts and turn back to my computer. I close out of the marketing report and check my email inbox. I'm surprised I don't have a snarky reply from Sandra about my reporting concerns.

If we keep seeing spam complaints at this level, we are at risk of being blacklisted and unable to send out any further emails. I don't even know what the procedure would be to reverse that.

I chew my lower lip. I wonder if someone accidentally imported bad data while adding new leads. It wouldn't be the first time someone from sales or marketing purchased a list of contacts online. Sometimes, spam traps are embedded in online lists to catch unethical marketing tactics.

Maybe it's all coincidental, and the number will level off in a week or two. Shoving my worry aside, I finish the last few tasks for the day and log out.

CHAPTER 8

The next morning, I lay on the floor of the bathroom, cursing my damnable luck. I am the epitome of despair as yet another misery is dropped on my head.

Why I thought I'd treat myself to sushi, I don't know. My stomach is still revolting 12 hours later.

I thought for sure the nausea would pass in the night, but alas, here I am, curled into the fetal position on the cold tile floor.

My chest aches from retching, and my bones have become brittle. I vaguely remember reading *Dante's Inferno*, but I'm not sure which circle of hell is responsible for my current predicament. Regardless, I'm positive that's where I am.

A gentle knock sounds on the door as Spencer steps inside as cautiously as one would enter a haunted house. Bless his heart, but he does not do well with any sort of bodily fluids.

"Hey," he says barely above a whisper, "How are you feeling this morning?"

My only response is a guttural groan.

The rabid monster that was my nausea last evening has lessened to a feral cat, slightly less ferocious but scrappy, nonetheless.

"I brought you some water," Spencer says, setting a glass on the bathroom counter before quickly stepping out of the room.

Coward.

* * *

My left leg bounces anxiously. After three days of never-ending nausea, I finally dragged my exhausted butt into the urgent care clinic. I can't keep living this way.

Soul-sucking depression? Sure. That, I can cope with. But I can't keep going to work, feeling ill at the briefest whiff of Shelby's reheated Thai food. Outside of a few salted pretzels and water, I've had nothing to eat all day. Even in my current warped state of mind, I realize I can't sustain this.

After what feels like a 2-day wait, I am ushered into an exam room painted in a sickly shade of green. Another eternity later, a middle-aged man in a navy scrub top and lab coat appears at the door.

"Hello, Mrs...." he says, glancing at my chart, "Swanson. What are we seeing you for today?"

His low, impersonal tone grates on my nerves.

"I think I have a bad case of food poisoning. I haven't been able to keep anything down for days, and I'm exhausted. I got a couple of California rolls from the Sushi Palace on 11th street, and I have been hurling ever since."

I realize now that I'm rambling and try to pump the brakes on my runaway mouth.

"Well, Taylor, I hate to break it to you, but the exhaustion and nausea are going to continue for a while." He says with the slightest hint of a smile.

"Sweetie," he says warmly, "You're pregnant."

The hands on the clock above his head freeze. All the air evaporates from the room, and the only sound is the thud of my heart. I feel a curious tickling sensation on my face, and with trembling fingers, I reach up to feel that my cheeks are damp.

Am I… am I crying?

"Pregnant?" I whisper.

"I'd guess you to be around 6 or 7 weeks along. You just need to set up a prenatal appointment with your OBGYN."

The doctor says something else, but I can't get over that one simple word: Pregnant.

"Okay. Well, if you don't need anything else, I'll show you out," he says awkwardly.

Somehow, I snap back to reality and nod in understanding.

"You can try a little ginger tea for that pesky nausea," he adds, chuckling softly, "That worked wonders for my wife back in the day."

I manage to mumble a barely audible "thanks" as he leads me down the hallway toward the reception area. Once there, he steps aside for me to pass.

"Oh, and one more thing," he says as I turn back to face him. "Congratulations, Mrs. Swanson."

Chapter 9

I have always avoided this corner of the store with pastel walls and racks of tiny clothes. It hurt too much, even passing near the baby section. But now there's a glow in my heart as I peruse the stacks of soft cotton pants and little onesies. I'm a bona fide expectant mother. Finally!

Rationally, I know it's early. I don't even know if I'm having a boy or a girl. But does it matter? My brain is screaming, "I'm having a baby!" over and over again.

I'm dropping outfit after outfit into my basket, already starting a mental checklist of all the things I'll need: Blankets. Crib. Bottles. Bulb Syringes. I'm prepared. I need to start a baby registry. And repaint the spare bedroom. And install a baby gate over the basement stairs. There's so much to do!

Looking at the small mountain of clothes I've collected, I decide that it's probably time to head to the checkout before I max out my credit card or clear out the entire store.

As I head toward the cash registers, I swing by the pharmacy section. The part of me that's still in denial needs one more bit of proof.

The ugly voice in the back of my head starts sowing seeds of doubt on the car ride home. What if the doctor was wrong? This joy just seems too fragile to be real.

Once I pull in the drive, I waste no time taking that cellophane-wrapped box straight to the bathroom. My fingers tremble in anticipation as I wait those dreaded 3 minutes. Taking several deep breaths, I attempt to steady my racing heart as I pick the plastic test up off the cool tile counter.

Positive.

I clap my hand over my mouth to stifle a shriek of joy. I mean, I *was* there when the doctor told me the news. But somehow it took this moment for it all to truly sink in. I can't recall how many times I've seen one line where there should've been two. It feels like the first time I finally managed to stay balanced on my bike after the training wheels came off.

As many times as I scraped my knees falling off that metal contraption, I've collapsed sobbing on this very floor.

In wonder, I carry the test to the kitchen and arrange it amongst the various items I purchased.

Taking a sip of ginger ale to settle the still-lingering nausea, I peek out the window. Spencer's truck comes rattling up the road.

Why am I suddenly so nervous? I swipe my sweaty palms on my jeans as I race to the front door to head him off.

"Hey!" Spencer says, surprised to see me greeting him. "What's for supper?"

"Why don't you go see for yourself," I say mischievously.

Cocking an eyebrow playfully, he steps around me and walks toward the kitchen.

"What's all this?" He gestures toward all the shopping bags

on the counter.

He stops, and I freeze as he takes everything in. He silently reaches for the pregnancy test and then gently lifts a baby shirt embroidered with the words "Hi Daddy." Spencer doesn't move. He doesn't make a sound.

Concerned, I come up beside him and place my hand on his back. Wordlessly, he pulls me into a tight hug.

"I can't believe it," he says with a voice choked by tears, "We've waited so long for this!"

As we both dissolve in each other's arms, I'm reminded of the first time we ever held each other after his father died. We weren't even friends at the time, but grief brought us together in a tearful embrace.

In all the years since, I have never seen him shed a tear. Until now.

Later that night, I walk to the living room and pick up the carved wood box on the bookshelf.

My happiness is welling up to the surface and breaking through the hardened layers of emotion that I've kept tamped down for all these years.

Feeling around in the dark, I pull out the knitted baby booties. To think that soon, these will be adorning a pair of tiny feet. Another silent tear slides down my face as I kiss the soft yarn.

I sigh with satisfaction as I turn and head down the hallway. Stepping into our spare room, I place them on the floor along with the other items I brought home from the store. Leaning back against the old dresser, I examine the room.

A fresh coat of paint is definitely in order. Maybe a pastel yellow? The old shades need to be replaced with a cute curtain. The crib could go along the north wall with the changing table beside it. Just like that, the nursery is taking shape before my eyes.

I envision a zoo theme, with giraffes and elephants in soft, neutral colors adorning the walls. I'd place a wooden rocking chair in the corner with a little bookshelf. And a sign above the crib for the name: Faith Marie, a tribute to my mother.

Or Chance Allen, but I'm positive it's a girl.

My heart squeezes at the thought of those names having a rightful owner at last. I place a hand against my belly, sending well wishes to the tiny embryo within.

"I can't wait to meet you, sweetheart," I whisper to my nonexistent bump. "I love you so much."

A half-forgotten country melody drifts into mind — about a girl with sky-colored eyes. I imagine my Faith with wispy blond locks and baby blue eyes.

Humming softly, I give the room a final wistful glance before clicking off the light and heading to bed.

* * *

Balloons. Check.

Absurd Decorations. Check.

Goofy birthday hats. Check.

Your husband only turns 30 once, and I am going all out. I mentally run through the list of things I have to do on Friday after work: pick up the cake from the bakery, get the decorations set up, and grab a box of tacos from his favorite food truck.

He's told me several times that he doesn't want me to "make a big deal about it," but I just can't help myself.

Hitting such an important milestone and becoming a father

in the same year is something to celebrate. Finally, we have something positive in our lives instead of the same old, same old. And he absolutely deserves to be spoiled.

What he doesn't know is that I have ordered a die-cast replica of Donna Sue, his original derby car. As much as I loathed that obnoxiously loud hunk of steel in the beginning, I have a few fond memories of watching him compete when we first started dating.

I still don't quite understand the appeal of intentionally beating the crap out of a car and then driving it around, crashing it into other beat-up cars. But people came out in droves to watch the annual Macon County Derby. Who knew the destruction of things could be so beloved?

I always sat on the edge of my seat, wound tighter than a spring with anxiety. The memory of the night Donna Sue started on fire still sends ice down my veins. Firefighters sprang from the dirt embankment into the arena to douse the flames that were licking the hood. I remember rushing from the grandstands with a hammering heart, terrified that Spencer wouldn't make it out. There was so much smoke that I couldn't even see the car. After the longest minute and a half of my life, Spencer emerged, flashing his typical boyish grin and blowing me a kiss.

Somehow, even Donna Sue made it through that fire relatively unscathed. He ran that old girl for two summers before the transmission blew up, and she was officially retired. Pieces and parts of her were robbed over the years for other derby cars until there was nothing left but the skeleton of a frame.

I know how much that car meant to him, as it was the last thing his father ever gave him before he passed away. It almost broke his heart when he finally gave in to his mama's nagging and hauled it to the scrap yard.

He's going to flip when he sees this little trinket. The car sits on a wooden pedestal with the words *Donna Sue* engraved on the front.

"Taylor!"

"Hmm?" I turn toward the sound of Jenna's voice.

"Did you hear the news?"

Puzzled, I give her a blank look.

"Shelby's knocked up!"

Glancing toward Shelby's unoccupied chair, I nod, knowing full well her absence this morning is due to an appointment with her OB. It's been three days since I found out my own good news, but I haven't had the chance to tell her yet. She's going to flip when she finds out we're both pregnant at the same time. I can't wait to see her face.

"Yeah, she mentioned that."

It kind of surprised me that Shelby confided in me before Jenna about the pregnancy. Granted, we've been working together longer, but the two of them used to close down the bar every weekend. I just assumed they were besties.

Jenna sidles over to my desk, and the look in her eye tells me she's mining for some juicy gossip.

"What kind of a mom do you think she'll be? She parties… like every weekend."

I ignore her comment, but she continues anyway, "Does she even know who the father is?"

The acid in her tone has me boiling. To call yourself a friend and then talk like this behind her back. I bite back the retort I have on the tip of my tongue and try to remain neutral.

"Who knows, people change when they have kids."

Jenna huffs and stalks off.

Her rudeness is a splinter under my skin. No one should judge Shelby's situation but her. Then the irritation dissolves into guilt because I, too, had the same thoughts mere weeks ago. I just didn't voice my opinion.

An incoming text pings my phone, providing the perfect distraction.

Sis! We must get together soon to chat about the bachelorette party! Much to discuss!

Oh boy. I do not have the energy for that right now. I type a vague response about meeting "sometime next week."

I don't know who decided that the matron of honor would be tasked with so many responsibilities. I have enough going on in my life right now. Groaning, I make a mental note to get Shelby's opinion on bachelorette party planning. I'm out of my league there.

I rest my hand on my lower abdomen. Despite the chaos surrounding me, I have a tiny miracle right here. It has only been a week, but this babe is already making me a frequent flyer at the ladies' room.

I rise from my chair and head toward my favorite bathroom stall — the one that is just the right distance from the door. My bladder practically sighs with relief.

But relief is not what I feel when I look down and see the water in the bowl is stained crimson.

Chapter 10

I've often observed Spencer clean fresh-caught trout. Their wet, shimmering bodies flopping across the cutting board, mouths opening and closing in desperation. It's a gruesome sight to behold as their bellies are sliced and their insides ripped out. That is how I feel right now.

Absolutely gutted.

Panic rises as I wipe, and the tissue comes back red. Blood red.

"No, no, no," I whisper frantically under my breath. "This can't be happening."

My mind goes black, and I have no idea what to do.

Terror grips me as I reach for the phone in my coat pocket, jabbing at the screen with trembling fingers until a familiar voice sounds on the other end of the line.

"I-I-I'm bleeding. I don't know what to do." I stammer.

My whole body is convulsing uncontrollably now.

"Breathe." Spencer's calming voice soothes through the phone.

I take a shaky breath, and then he launches into fixing mode. "Tell me what's going on. Do you need me to come get you? Have you called your doctor?"

His last remark sets me off.

"I don't need a damn doctor to tell me I'm losing my baby!" I hurl the words like a weapon.

I clamp my hand over my mouth in shock at what just came out. At that, I begin to sob as my world crumbles around me.

I end the call and sink to the floor of the bathroom. For a single moment, I allow myself to come unglued. An unrelenting wall of pain slams into me, and I let myself feel every last ounce of it.

After the moment has passed, I gather my composure, clean myself up, and exit the bathroom.

I head toward my desk just as Sandra steps out of the general manager's office. I hang my head to avoid eye contact, but it's too late. She has me in her crosshairs.

"Swanson, you've been slacking off as of late. Spending a bit too much time 'in the ladies room.'" She waggles her fingers in air quotes on the last part as if it's a cover for some suspicious activity.

The constant inner urge to be polite wrestles with my emotional upheaval. I open my mouth to smart off, but clamp my lips shut and continue past her. This seems to infuriate her even more.

"Excuse me, I was talking to you!"

I pause midstride, still unable to bring words to mind as she continues her scolding.

"Your latest report was atrocious, Swanson. You need to clean up those numbers before corporate comes sniffing around. I expect a new report on my desk by end of day!"

As if my work has ever been anything but flawless. Heat rises within me, and I feel myself on the verge of snapping.

Whipping around, I take a challenging step toward her.

"First of all," I manage to say with authority, "My name is Taylor, and my report is not wrong. Run the numbers yourself. I'm taking the rest of the day off."

Not bothering to stay and watch the smug look melt off her face, I turn back to my cubicle and grab my purse. I march to the exit, only hearing bits and pieces of her flabbergasted response.

"This is very unprofessional, *Taylor*. There's a protocol in place for requesting PTO!"

The energy blazing through me from my office outburst drains the second I get in my car and drown.

I silence about 12 calls from Spencer as I speed home through a blur of tears. He's already there when I pull into the driveway.

Concern mars his perfect face as he opens my door and pulls me to his chest.

"Baby, talk to me. What's going on?" he murmurs in my ear.

"I lost her. I lost her. I lost her." I sob into the front of his stained work shirt.

"Shhh..."

He leads me into the house and settles me onto the couch. After draping a knitted blanket over me and bringing me water, he rushes to the bedroom. Through the wall, I hear him on the phone with Dr. Jensen, but I only catch bits and pieces of the conversation.

"What are the signs of infection?"

"Okay, I'll keep an eye on her.."

"...and this should all pass in a few days?"

"...I'll bring her in if anything changes."

I curl into a ball and squeeze my eyes shut to block everything out. Mercifully, I drift off to a dreamless sleep.

* * *

The next morning, I wake to a note from Spencer.

"I've texted your boss that you were going to be out sick today. Please take care of yourself. Call me if you need anything. There's breakfast in the microwave. I love you. – Spencer."

I swallow the bile rising in my throat as the smell of bacon still lingers over the stove. As I pop open the microwave, I get one whiff of the plate of food he left and immediately slam the door shut again. Whipping around, I start dry heaving into the kitchen trash can.

The garbage is nearly overflowing. The one thing Spencer is supposed to take care of around here. Pushing through the nausea, I remove the bag and take it to the bin outside. While I'm throwing things away, I might as well go through everything.

I propel myself into the spare bedroom. Boxes of diapers, clothes, and toys have accumulated here as I've prepared the nursery items.

Cold, hard pain spears my chest as I gather everything together, tucking it away in the back of the closet to be left and forgotten.

But how can I possibly forget?

The doorbell ringing stops me in my tracks. Peering out the window, I see a delivery driver briskly walking back to his truck. Spencer's gift has arrived.

Retrieving it from the porch, I suddenly remember the plans I had for this weekend. This wasn't supposed to happen! I had planned such a special evening. We were supposed to celebrate. The unfairness of it all grips me, and I fall to my knees in sobs.

In a fit of anger, I shove the package into the closet alongside all the other items I'll no longer need. While I'm at it, I find the box of things I use to hurt myself, and I pack it in as well. I just want to lock this door and make everything behind it disappear forever. I furiously swipe the tears from my eyes.

Why am I so weak? So hopeless? Useless? Emotion ricochet around my brain like bullets and I can't grasp a single one.

In a manic state, I begin cleaning everything, dusting the top of the entertainment center, erasing each mark from the baseboards, and scrubbing the kitchen tiles until blisters appear on my palms.

Unaware of the hours ticking by, I hurry from task to task with trembling hands. Anything to keep my mind from what is happening. It is in this frenzied state that Spencer finds me when he steps through the kitchen door.

He looks at me like I'm a spooked colt he's trying to tame.

"Taylor?"

Pots and pans are clanging around as I reorganize the cabinet for the second time. I got everything just how I wanted it. But while unloading the dishwasher, I found another skillet. Now, nothing is lining up the way I had it.

I should just throw all these pans away and buy new ones. The nonstick coating is peeling off half of them, and there are rust stains on the bottom of my good ones.

The hell with it! I should throw all my utensils away as well! I grab a handful from the still-open drawer beside me and march toward the trash can. I drop them in without a second thought and whip back toward the upheaval that is my kitchen.

I catch a glimpse of Spencer as I return to sorting pots and pans that are now spilling all over the floor. There is fear behind his eyes. Perfectly buttoned up, Taylor is falling apart, and he can't handle it.

"Why don't you go see Dr. Jensen. Maybe there's something she can do," he pleads.

Anger courses through me like molten lava.

"Like what, Spencer?" I snap, "Bring my baby back from the dead?"

His mouth falls open at the ruthlessness of my comment. For a moment, we just stare at each other, and then he presses his lips together in a tight line and walks away.

I hurt him, and I know it. He's grieving too, but right now, I don't give a damn. It's *my* body that isn't doing what it should be doing. I'm the failure here, and I can't deal with his disappointment. It's crippling.

My spine dissolves, and I crumple to the floor like a wet bath towel. I scream until I can't catch my breath, but no tears come. My baby is gone forever, and maybe so am I.

* * *

My head feels like someone stuffed it full of dryer lint, and my stomach is on tumble dry. I peel my eyelids open to glance at the clock. It's almost 6, and Spencer will be home soon. Not that he'll speak to me. He's been giving me a wide berth all weekend since my blow-up in the kitchen Friday night.

Not sure why he's suddenly volunteering for the weekend shift, but my money is on avoidance. He's never been able to handle any sort of conflict, so instead of digging in, he walks away. Not that we've ever faced anything like this before.

Groaning, I roll onto my side, snuggling my face back into

the couch cushions. If only I could dissolve into the fibers and become one with the sofa. I would never have to leave. I would never have to work again. Or eat. Or breathe.

But the never-ending drive to get up and go still pulses beneath my skin. Unfortunately. I wish I could silence that damn voice that never lets me rest.

I'm dreading work tomorrow. My stomach pitches just imagining Sandra's fury. Shelby has texted a few times asking how I'm feeling. She thinks I'm recovering from a nasty case of food poisoning. Little does she know...

Spencer shuffles into the kitchen door with two arms full of bags.

"I bought a few groceries," he mumbles, "And I picked up a few subs from that deli you like. Since... you know...you can have that again."

"Really, Spencer?" I look at him sharply.

"Okay, I'm sorry," he says, seeing the blind rage on my face, "I was just trying to do something nice."

Some part of me knows he's trying, but I can't deal with it right now. Anger has me in its firm grasp. Instead, I flee to the bedroom and slam the door.

* * *

"Okay. Thanks, Dr. Jensen," I say politely before ending the call.

I open the stall door and peek out, ensuring I'm still alone. I take a deep breath and close my eyes.

It has been a week and a half of constant bleeding, and I'm getting a little concerned. Dr. Jensen says it is rare for a miscarriage to last this long, but it is possible. So far, I'm not experiencing any symptoms of hemorrhage or infection, so she's not overly concerned. But she repeatedly offered to schedule an exam to check on things for my *peace of mind*.

Peace of mind? I think we're a little beyond that point. Maybe I'm even in denial. Going to the clinic only to be faced with a dark, empty ultrasound will just make it all final. Knowing she's gone is worse than the actual bleeding.

I fight back the urge to cry and instead turn the faucet on and let the warm water flow over my ice-cold fingers. Glancing up, I stare at the woman in the mirror. I don't even recognize myself anymore. I haven't been in this much emotional agony since my mother's death.

I remember all the empty condolences that were doled out to me at the time. The well-meaning expressions felt more like a slap in the face to my teenage self.

"She's in a better place."

"At least she isn't in pain anymore."

"You'll see her again someday."

Everything fell flat. I didn't want words of comfort. I wanted my mom, and she was gone forever. I didn't want people's pity. I wanted to be left alone. Now I feel the same way.

Only this time, no one is waiting with a sympathetic word. It's just me carrying the burden of grief alongside a husband who feels a million miles away.

What a pair we are, two lost souls drawn to each other through grief. Now our shared misery will be what tears us apart.

A noise interrupts my thoughts as the bathroom door swings open. Shelby smiles brightly as she hurries past me.

"I swear I'm in here more than I am at my desk these days," she jokes, swinging the door shut behind her.

I grimace and turn off the tap, flicking the excess water into the basin. Moments later, there's a flush, and she emerges from the stall. Shelby stops short and cocks her head.

"Are you okay? You've seemed a little off lately."

"Me? I'm fine," I lie, grabbing a paper towel and slowly drying my hands.

Shelby's perfectly manicured brows furrow as she studies me.

"You know you can tell me if something is bothering you, right?"

A vice tightens around my heart.

Tell her the truth.

But I can't do that. It would only make her feel bad for me. I don't want her pity.

"Nah, I think I'm just coming down with something."

She shrugs and leans over to wash her hands. "Again? Ugh. That sucks. Well, don't mind me if I keep my distance. Last thing I need is to catch something."

I clench my teeth to avoid a nasty response.

"You know," she continues blissfully unaware that she's digging a dagger into me.

"I hear you can't even take cold medicine while pregnant."

I nod once, bury the jealousy six feet deep, and stride out of the bathroom.

* * *

One of these days, I will become permanently fused to this couch. There will be a Taylor-sized divot in the cushions when they pry my cold, dead carcass off the fabric. My gut feels like it is already beginning to rot. My hair hasn't been washed in days and is hanging in greasy strands around my face.

I've been wallowing for three weeks. Still bleeding. Still grieving. When is this going to end?

To date, I have called Dr. Jensen three times, run at least 100 Google searches, and taken two pregnancy tests. Both tests came back positive, which Dr. Jensen has categorized as rare but not unheard of, due to the lingering amounts of HCG in my bloodstream. She keeps reminding me that getting checked in the clinic would be best, but she's respecting my decision to wait this out.

At this point, I'm not even sure what I'm waiting for. I know this isn't rational, but every time I think about going to the clinic, I can't breathe.

Part of me just wants to book the appointment to get it over with. But what are they going to tell me that I don't already know? In the meantime, I've memorized all the warning signs and symptoms. I have never spent more time on Google than I have these past few days. Outside of "taking it easy," there has been no advice on how to speed this along.

Losing my baby this way is like ripping my heart out every single day and sprouting a new one every morning just to start the cycle anew. If this miscarriage could end, maybe I could pull myself together and try to move on. Maybe then I could repair this thing with Spencer.

Yesterday, while lying nauseated on the bathroom floor, Spencer came in from work to take a shower. I snapped at him for tracking mud in the house, and when he looked at me, I didn't see the charming glint in his eyes anymore. They just looked bloodshot, and he looked at me like he didn't even know me.

"If you're this miserable," he said flatly, "then why don't you go to the doctor instead of lashing out at me?"

My fiery rage fizzled out with his remark. I know I've been punishing him for the pain I'm in. But I don't have anything left inside me but anger. I'm nothing.

Stop feeling sorry for yourself!

I muster the strength to pull myself up off the couch, only to freeze with utter horror.

This whole time, I've been lying in a pool of blood.

"Hey," Spencer says cautiously, walking in from the kitchen.

I don't even hear him approach. My brain is hyper-focused on the contrasting red stain seeping into the light grey fabric of the couch.

From out of nowhere, the words of my mother's favorite song echo in the back of my mind. A haunting George Strait ballad about a girl arriving soft as spring and disappearing without reason.

Chapter 11

Hospital gowns are not for the cold-blooded. I shiver under the thin cotton as the on-call ultrasound tech prepares for my exam.

Internally, I am seething that Spencer insisted on dragging me here. His face had drained of all color at the sight of so much blood, and he immediately rushed me into the car. I was so numb, I didn't have it in me to fight him.

I've just been along for the ride, barely aware of my surroundings until this moment. Now I'm on high alert. My last ultrasound was not a walk in the park, and I am not looking forward to where that wand is about to go.

The nurse is asking questions about when my miscarriage started and so on. Spencer has mostly been doing the talking thing for me. Thank God. Words do not come easily to me in times of crisis.

I react with due diligence when asked to "scoot down on the table. A little more. A little more. Now open your knees."

I hate everything about this. I don't want to be here.

Agonizing thoughts prey on my feeble brain like a predator. If only I could will myself away to some magical land where babies don't die.

I turn my head to finally look at Spencer, who gives me a tender look and gently squeezes my hand – the same one he hasn't let go of since we arrived. I'm suddenly so grateful that he's here. I don't think I can do this alone.

I revert my gaze to the ceiling and try to dissociate from what is happening. My whole world is about to be shredded.

As the procedure begins, I fight the urge to roll my eyes as the tech feeds me the whole "you're going to feel a little pressure" line.

Pressure, my ass.

"Hmm..." the ultrasound tech mumbles, moving the wand from side to side. "Looks like you're still pregnant," she says mechanically, "Would you like to hear the heartbeat?"

What?

Did I hear her right? I practically leap off the table as I turn to look at Spencer. With wide, unblinking eyes, he reaches for my hand and gives it a tender squeeze.

Seconds later, the room fills with the rapid whooshing of a fetal heart.

"Heartbeat sounds great," The tech says with a smile. "I'm going to do some measurements, and then the doctor will pop in."

I am utterly dazed but manage to nod enthusiastically. An embarrassing tear streaks across my cheek before I can wipe it away with the back of my hand.

The tech continues her work, pointing out different parts of the baby's anatomy as she goes. She is "Oooing" and "Awwing" over every adorable feature. But to me, the fuzzy black and white image on the screen appears to be nothing more than pools of ink flowing into one another. But then again, I'm in total shock, and nothing is making much sense right now.

I can't make out one blob from another, but somehow, there must be a baby in there. A baby with two arms, two legs, and a perfectly beating heart. My own thuds deep within my chest. My baby. My perfect tiny baby is alive!

Panic surges in my mind. What is going on? How is she alive? Is she *actually* a she?

"Do you know if it's a boy or a girl?" My voice breaks through the cacophony of my internal monologue.

"It's a little too early to tell." The ultrasound tech explains, "You could opt for the NPT blood test or wait until the 20-week ultrasound."

That was probably a stupid question, but I sense from her reflexive response that it's a commonly asked one. She finishes her work, pops off her gloves, and exits the room after reassuring us that the doctor will see us shortly.

Spencer and I wait in the deafening silence, both of us trying to wrap our brains around what has just transpired. What could all this mean? Why am I bleeding? Is the baby going to survive? Oh God, is she in pain?

Those questions cut me to the quick. Pressing my hand to my abdomen, I lift up a silent prayer to save this unborn life.

Minutes pass like hours, but eventually, Dr. Jensen's perky persona enters the room. Something feels off. Although her usual smile is plastered on her face, it feels like one of those cheap Halloween masks from the 80s. There's a darkness behind her eyes that unnerves me.

"Baby looks great." Dr. Jensen begins. "Strong fetal heartbeat around 155, everything is measuring on track, and I'd place you at 8 weeks, 5 days."

It sounds like she's ticking items off a list, and I sense there is a *but* coming.

She pulls up the ultrasound image on the screen and begins pointing things out in the murky grey tones that I can't wrap my mind around.

"Do you see this large black space here?" she asks rhetorically before continuing. "That is a subchorionic hematoma or a pocket of blood in your uterus."

"What does that mean?" Spencer pipes up beside me. "Will Taylor be okay?"

Dr. Jensen stops and turns back toward us with a concerned look on her face.

"Taylor is in no danger." She pauses, "But this could potentially be fatal for the baby."

She continues to explain more about the condition, but my mind is stuck on that word: fatal.

"This occurs more often than you'd think in a pregnancy, but they are typically small and dissolve on their own. They don't cause any issues outside of a little spotting. But I've never seen anything like this before."

Great. I love being a rare exception to the rule. I'm thrilled. I take a breath as my internal sarcasm bleeds into panic.

"The concern is that if this pooling of blood continues to expand, it will tear the placenta away from the wall of the uterus and terminate the pregnancy."

My head hangs as I try to understand what is happening. Spencer is the first to brave the silence.

"What are our chances?"

Dr. Jensen takes a seat on the exam stool and meets my eyes.

"I'm not going to sugarcoat it for you. It doesn't look

good. However, baby's vitals are excellent, which makes me cautiously optimistic. But the reality is that you have about a 50/50 chance of getting this baby to term."

Inhaling deeply to steady my nerves, I gather the courage to speak my greatest fear.

"Did I do this?" I ask in a wavering voice.

"Absolutely not," she says firmly. "We have no idea what causes a hematoma to occur, and there's nothing we can do about it once it does."

"But I should have come in weeks ago," I protest weakly. "I-I didn't know."

"It wouldn't have mattered." She gives my knee a reaffirming squeeze. "It wasn't your fault, Taylor."

I nod through the tears streaming shamelessly down my face now. I still feel guilty. Nothing can erase that.

"Now I want you to take it easy for the next few days," she has switched back to business, "Come back in on Monday, and we'll do another scan to see what we're dealing with. Best case scenario, the pooling has receded, and we can continue with our prenatal workup."

The worst-case scenario remains unsaid, but I can tell from the energy in the room that it lies heavily on everyone's mind.

After she leaves, Spencer leans into me, and the emotions fall over us like a weighted curtain. Or worse, an executioner's axe.

* * *

"Hey, you made it!" a half-drunk bridesmaid hoots the following night.

Of course, I made it. I *planned* this shindig over the last few miserable weeks. Now this is the last place I actually want to be, but obligation dragged me here.

Well. To be fair, Shelby did the vast majority of the brainstorming, and I just implemented it. I am no party girl, and I don't know the first thing about planning a bachelorette party. I never had one, considering I had zero female friends and wasn't old enough to drink.

Fortunately, my work wife had all the best advice to give. She gave me notes on the best bars and clubs to hit up, plus some great gift ideas. I treated Leslie to a nice spa day and a mani/pedi before dinner at Michele's Steakhouse.

But this part of the evening I have been dreading. Dancing and drinking are not my typical hobbies. I hate getting dressed up, I am terrible at hair and makeup, and I can't stand clubs.

But I'm doing my best to play the part of a good matron of honor despite Dr. Jensen's order of "taking it easy." I put on the only dress I own that can pass for cocktail attire and then tried and failed to recreate a smoky eye from some online makeup tutorial. I swapped the teeny tiny heels I had previously planned to wear for some obnoxiously glittery sandals. I can't walk in heels on a good day, and I'm certainly not risking a broken ankle in my current situation. The fear of harming my unborn baby lurks constantly in my mind.

How am I going to survive this night without alcohol? Gritting my teeth, I make my way to the bar, sidestepping past Leslie's drunken entourage.

Making sure the group is out of earshot, I order a cherry mocktail and pray I won't look suspicious. I do *not* need anyone asking questions tonight.

Leslie sidles up beside me at the bar and orders two shots of vodka. She looks trashed already. Platinum strands are falling out of her perfectly sculpted updo, her eyes look bleary beneath her fluttery lashes, and her obnoxious glow-in-the-dark BRIDE sash keeps falling off her left shoulder. Despite her ruddy cheeks and rising blood-alcohol level, she still looks gorgeous.

When our drinks arrive, she throws me a wide grin and slides a shot towards me across the polished bar top.

"To the best matron of honor ever," she slurs, manicured nails clinking against her raised shot glass.

She glances expectantly at the drink in front of me.

"Oh no, sis," I huff, pushing the glass away, "You know I don't do vodka."

She rolls her eyes, "Don't give me that *'I'm a beer girl'* crap." She breaks into a fit of giggles before she continues. "You're obviously keen on the cocktails."

Leslie motions to the glorified fruit juice concoction in my hand. Crap. I should have just ordered an NA beer, but they're so gross. Way to fly under the radar.

"Just let loose and have fun for once, Taylor," Leslie whines.

My brain flounders for a way out of this situation.

"That's alright, Les." I say in my best big sister voice, "You have a good time. This is your day."

"Shot, shot, shot…" she starts to chant.

"No, no. I'm good, thanks," I say, my cheeks flaming as other bridesmaids begin to chant along with her.

There's no way to leave this situation with any sort of dignity. I obviously can't drink the shot, but I can't politely decline without saying why. I clearly can't tell them I'm pregnant. Not when my baby's life hangs in such a precarious balance.

My eyes dart back and forth as the gaggle of girls seems to close in on me. I can't breathe under the rising pressure as others in the bar join in. Higher and higher, like a tidal wave about to crash over my head. Suddenly, I feel something burst within me, and I can take the mortification no more.

Heart racing, I barrel past Leslie's evil horde and bolt for the bathroom. I throw open the first stall, clawing through my patent leather clutch. Without thinking, I panic-dial the first number in my phone contacts.

"I need you to come get me," I blurt as soon as the drowsy voice picks up on the other end.

I hold my breath until I hear the muffled reply. "I'll be right there," Shelby says.

I hide out in the bathroom for 10 minutes until she texts that she's out front. Mercifully, I manage to circumvent Leslie's bridal party as I sneak out of the club and climb into Shelby's car.

She drives with one hand on the ever-so-slight bulge of her stomach and the other on the wheel. I can tell she wants desperately to say something, but doesn't. I'm not sure why I didn't call Spencer. He's already so keyed up about the baby, I figured calling him desperately for a ride home would send him into a panic. This way, I can slip in while he's asleep and he won't be the wiser. I suppose I could have always called an Uber, but somehow I just needed a friend.

"Thanks, Shelb," I say as she pulls up in front of my house.

"Any time." She says, smiling tightly at me. "Sorry, your night sucked."

She squeezes my hand before I open the car door and walk away. I don't deserve a friend like her.

Once inside, I hang my key on the peg by the door, slip off my shoes, and tiptoe through the house. As suspected, Spencer is passed out on his side of the bed, legs twitching like a sleeping puppy. The corner of my mouth lifts in a half smile as I pull back the covers and slide in beside him.

***

"Taylor."

My name is an echo followed by the low buzzing of electronic equipment.

A hand stretches out toward me like the Grim Reaper's grasp.

Fear takes hold as a scream cuts through the stillness.

Arms encircle my waist, tugging me further into the darkness.

"Please let me stay with her!" I wail and thrash against the figure behind me, desperately trying to free myself.

From somewhere in the room comes the sound of an infant's cry.

The tone of a flatline fills the room, and I collapse.

***

I'm ripped from sleep by the sensation of falling and instantly bolt off the mattress. It takes a moment to catch my breath and settle my racing pulse. Immediately, Spencer is there. His arms wrap around my shoulders, and he gently tows me back onto the bed.

"Shhhh," he soothes, pressing a kiss to the top of my head.

My skin is cold from the sweat that has me drenched, and I shiver against him. I press my hand to my eyes, trying to scrub the image of my dying mother from my mind.

I'm not sure what is worse, the nightmare itself or the aftermath. This particular dream has been haunting me since I was a teenager. They lessened considerably after Spencer, and I started dating, disappearing altogether for the first few years we were married.

Once my infertility issues began, the nightmare returned — slightly altered, but with the same withered hand reaching out and the strange arms cinching tight around me. It has been a nightly torment since my bleeding began. I assume it was made worse by the incident at Leslie's party.

Another shudder pulses through me, and Spencer tightens his embrace. He murmurs against my ear, "It's just the pregnancy hormones. This phase will pass."

I can only hope he's right in that assumption, and the dream isn't an ominous premonition. It is getting increasingly harder to recover, and the lack of sleep is taking a toll.

"I need some air," I mutter, dragging myself out of his arms and through the tangle of sheets and blankets.

I vigorously rub my arms to lessen the prickling of goosebumps that have cropped up in the cool night air. Staggering blindly, I make my way to the kitchen, pulling open the refrigerator door. I wince against the blinding LED light and blink a few times before I can make out the contents within.

I reach for the carton of orange juice and take a swig, not bothering with a glass for once in my life.

Taking the rest of the juice, I pull up a barstool and sit against the counter. I can't help but feel like the other shoe is about to drop. My troubled mind latches onto that phrase. I wonder just where that expression came from. Needing a distraction anyway, I reach for my phone and pull up a Google search page.

I type my question while shuffling to my reading nook and settling in. I take another drink of orange juice straight from the carton, skimming the initial results.

Moments later, I'm entrenched in an article about late 19th-

century tenements in New York City.

"With apartments built with bedrooms on top of one another, it was common to hear your upstairs neighbor take off a shoe, drop it, and then repeat the action."

So that is how it became associated with waiting for something you knew was going to happen. I just keep reminding myself of Dr. Jensen's words. Cautiously optimistic. It couldn't hurt to start looking at the bright side a little more.

I rest my hand on my still-flat tummy to ease a sudden wave of nausea.

"You'll be okay," I whisper, "Mommy's here, and you're not going anywhere."

Now that the churning in my gut has abated, I take my juice and mosey over to my reading nook. Absently, I take the faded leather journal down off the shelf and page through the first few entries until I find where I left off.

August 2, 1994

I can't believe how fast my baby is growing. Little Taylor is one month old today and is simply the sweetest thing I've ever seen. She has the littlest tufts of soft brown hair coming in. I wonder if it will lighten over time to match mine or remain like her father's.

I think a lot about who she will become someday. Will she be soft and gentle or brash and outspoken? Will she chase the butterflies in the flower garden or spend her days with a book of fables and a cup of tea? I hope she is everything. I hope she does whatever she sets out to do with a heart full of courage and kindness.

I hope she meets someone who is her equal in every way. Who loves her unconditionally for everything that she is, and I hope she has a life full of love and happiness. I can't wait for my darling girl to make all her dreams come true.

I am jolted awake by a sharp stab of pain.

For a second, I'm disoriented. I must have fallen asleep reading my mother's journal.

My hand flies to my lower abdomen as I'm hit with another. I groan and try to pull myself upright. In the process of righting myself, I tip over the still-open carton of orange juice.

Swearing, I try to make it to the kitchen for a towel to clean the sticky mess. After a few steps, I'm overcome by another shockwave of pain.

Something's not right.

Crying out, I lean forward with my hand on the wall, waiting for the pain to pass. Hearing my distress, Spencer rushes into the room. His eyes are wide with fear in the low light.

"Taylor?"

"Help me to the bathroom," I say through clenched teeth, holding out my arm.

He braces his strong body against mine, guiding me down the hallway. I wince with every step, trying to contain my panic.

Lowering myself onto the stool, I pull one knee to my chest in hopes of relieving the agony. Tears slip down my face as Spencer rifles through the medicine cabinet.

"I did some research," he says. "Tylenol should be safe for the baby."

He drops two capsules out of a bottle and holds out a glass of water with trembling hands.

I lower my leg and glance down to see a blood clot the size of my fist resting at the bottom of the bowl, and a sense of horror envelops me.

"Spencer, I'm scared," I whisper as a knot forms in my throat.

"I got you," he says, meeting my eyes.

I cling to that promise as he helps me into the car, buckles me in, and speeds to the hospital. The lights from the city blur past, but I can only focus on one thing.

The cramps continue to hit me in varying degrees of intensity. Some feel like a quick pinch, while others wash over me with a crashing wave, leaving me feeling like I've been licked by flames. I have been holding Spencer's arm in a death grip, but he doesn't even seem to notice.

His eyes never leave the road. He's terrified. And whatever he's feeling, I feel threefold. At long last, the hospital comes into view, and he whips into the closest parking stall.

I feebly make my way into the lobby, where he takes over again. He explains the situation to the nurses on call while I wait in absolute misery. Finally, he returns and drops into the seat next to me, and we wait.

A nurse quickly appears and ushers us down a maze of hallways to an exam room. Once again, I let Spencer answer all the questions.

"Can you tell me about your pain, Taylor?" the nurse prods.

I guess Spencer can't do all the talking for me.

I do my best to summarize the cramps that come and go. She nods, typing something into the tablet in her hand.

"We're going to page Dr. Jensen, and she'll meet you in radiology."

She gives some brief instructions on the location of said department, and now it's my turn to nod numbly as we fumble out of the room. Somehow, Spencer navigates us to the east wing of the hospital, up the elevator, and into yet another waiting area.

Everything is moving at a rapid pace, yet I'm oblivious to it all. This wait is much shorter, and we're only seated for a few minutes before we are escorted to the ultrasound suite.

I'm given the same instructions to prep for the scan, and I comply. My heart begins to pound as Dr. Jensen enters the room.

"I hear you're having some cramps and clotting. We'll take a peek here and see what's going on," she says in an upbeat voice, "Hopefully, this is just some of that bleeding passing through."

"Okay," I mutter.

"When was your last cramp?" she asks, glancing at her watch.

It's then that I realize I haven't had one since we arrived in the ER.

"Um," I say, looking to Spencer for confirmation, "about half an hour?"

She hmms as she slips into a pair of latex gloves. Trying to muster up some courage, I brace myself for the probe. If there is a god in the world, please let Dr. Jensen be right. It's just the hematoma. The baby is okay.

I grit my teeth and stare at the screen, watching all those black-and-white blobs shift and swirl with the movement of the wand. I see shapes and shadows, but most of the screen is black. I can't make anything out. No vague shapes of arms, or legs, or faces appear.

No heartbeat sounds.

Keep looking. Please, she has to be there. I want to scream.

My teeth catch my bottom lip as Dr. Jensen turns from the monitor to face me. She doesn't have to say anything. Her brows furrow, and deep creases appear around her eyes as she finally speaks.

"I'm so sorry, Taylor. I'm afraid you've miscarried."

I don't hear anything else in the room after that.

Chapter 12

I flip to the back of my mom's journal and find a single empty page. On a whim, I grab a pen from the desk and pour out my heart. My hand shakes as the pen scrapes across the lined page.

April 6, 2022

My dearest Faith,

I don't know how to say goodbye. It seems one moment, I was singing an old George Strait song to you, and then suddenly, you were gone. My precious little baby. I can't come to terms with knowing you were here one minute and gone the next. You meant everything to your daddy and me.

We were so happy, and now I don't know exactly what I'm going to do. I blame myself — if only I had protected you more somehow, maybe this all could have been avoided.

I know it wasn't meant to be, but that doesn't make this any easier. My heart breaks that I'll never get to know you, but you will never be forgotten. Go be with the angels, little one.

I may have only been your mom for a little while, but no one can ever take that away from me. You'll always be my baby blue.

I will love and miss you for all my days.

Love,

Mom

I close the journal and set it aside. All those words of love from an absent mother, followed by an entry of sorrow for a child who is lost forever. The irony of it all leaves a bitter taste in my mouth. I try to swallow, but my emotions have closed off my throat.

I keep reliving the other night in the exam room as Dr. Jensen held my hand and let me cry. She reassured me that I didn't cause this and that coming in sooner wouldn't have helped. But nothing will assuage my guilt.

My breaths begin coming at a rapid pace, and I can't seem to get enough oxygen down in my lungs. I scramble to my feet in a blind panic.

Spencer. I need Spencer.

I need him to rush in with a cool glass of water and that soothing voice to ease the pain.

But it's Monday, and he's at work. I'm alone here.

At last, a sob bursts from my chest and breaks through the hyperventilation. I collapse on the floor next to the window seat, and my body begins to convulse.

"Why did this happen?" I scream, "Why me?"

The universe sends no response. I dig my palms into my eyes as hard as I can to staunch the flow of tears, but it's futile. Instead, I wrap my arms around my knees and rock back and forth, moaning.

"What did I do wrong?" I mumble.

But that is one thing no soul can answer.

Why did I live, but my baby died? In what universe is that fair?

Then, from the dark abyss of my mind, a voice whispers, *"Maybe you were never cut out to be a mother."*

And that cuts me to the quick.

* * *

"Earth to Taylor!"

My head snaps to attention, and I peel off my headphones and spin around in my chair. Shelby looms over my desk with a puzzled look on her face.

"Where have you been?" she asks.

"What do you mean? I've been here all day."

"I mean up in there," she says, jabbing my head with her index finger.

"Ow," I whine, rubbing my temple.

"Spill. You were out again yesterday, and you look like shit today."

Apparently, I wear depression like a neon sign.

"Nothing, just some personal stuff," I mutter.

"So, you're either dying of cancer or your relationship is on the rocks," she says, studying me.

I give her an irritated look. "Okay, so not dying," she says, taking a seat on my desk. "Ooo, is Spencer cheating?"

"No!" I snap.

"Alright, alright, settle down." She lifts her hands in surrender. "But you know you have to tell me these things. I'm dying for drama right now."

I resist the urge to roll my eyes.

"Oh, and you never did tell me what went down at the

bachelorette party," Shelby probes.

"It just was too much for me," I shrug, non-committal.

She narrows her eyes as if zeroing in on my insecurities, and I try not to shrivel under her gaze.

"Well, you didn't seem wasted, so what's up?"

"Oh, trust me. I wasn't the drunk one."

"Ah, Gotcha." She says, snapping her fingers, "Leslie's a mean drunk, eh?"

Weary, I run my hand over my face, "Something like that, I guess."

"That really sucks, dude," she sympathizes, "Has she reached out since?"

"Let's just say Leslie has little memory of that night."

The only text I'd received just thanked me for planning the party and questioned why I left early. Either she doesn't recall the humiliation she put me through, or she simply doesn't care. Either way, I wasn't going to bring it up and replied with a simple "No problem."

"That's a major bummer," Shelby says.

Her hand falls to the swell of her belly, and my stomach churns. It's not quite a bump yet. If you didn't know she was pregnant, you wouldn't even notice the slight curve of her stomach. She gives it a gentle caress before hopping off my desk and returning to her own.

"You know it's funny," she says, turning back to me, "Now I am living vicariously through *you*. Huh!"

Acid burns in my gut as I step toward the bathroom. I need to compose myself and retighten the lid on my carefully contained emotions.

"Oh, and you're coming Friday night, right?"

I wrack my brain, trying to remember what she's talking

about. Instead, I bob my head dumbly.

"Okay, great! I'm so excited to find out if I'm having a boy or girl! Eee!" she squeals gleefully.

If I don't step away now, I just might vomit all over her perfect, floral dress.

"Right. Can't wait." I mutter before dashing away.

* * *

I tug a brush through my damp tresses, scowling at the rat's nest on my head. Catching another knot, I grimace, and I rip the bristles through the tangled strands. I could just give up right now.

I could leave my hair a matted mess, let moss grow on my head, and live in a ditch.

Ditch people don't have to dress up, play pretend, and act nice. That game is for children. And apparently, adults who don't know how to set boundaries. Adults like me: Too afraid to tell the world to screw itself and spend too much time worrying that someone might not like me.

I loathe makeup. No matter how many tutorials I watch, I always manage to look like a painted doll. One of those old porcelain types with exaggerated rosy cheeks and too-bright lips. Instead of looking glamorous or even sweet and subtle, I appear more like a horror movie villain.

Having no coordination whatsoever in my wrists, I can't seem to get my eyeliner even on both sides. My right eye looks like I have a shiner, and the left has barely a hint of black across my waterline.

In a fit of fury, I fling the pencil at the mirror, leaving an angry black line across my reflection. I reach for a towel and scrub at my face. The effort makes my eyes sting, and unshed tears threaten to flow.

Looking even more haunted with dark smudges encircling my eyes, I abandon the effort and dunk my face into the flow of the faucet. Black water drips down my cheeks before I bury my face in the towel.

Let's try this again.

Spencer taps on the door just as I'm finishing up. I am settling for a whiff of light brown eye shadow with a touch of mascara, a dab of concealer to hide some blemishes, and lightly tinted lip balm.

"Do I look like a clown?"

"Of course not," Spencer says from the doorway.

Still frowning at my reflection and toying with my still-drying waves, I am barely aware of him taking my wrist and placing a gentle kiss on the back of my hand.

"Look at me," he says, firmly tugging at my arm.

I turn to face him expectantly.

"Taylor, you are the most beautiful woman. I love you."

My fractured heart skips a beat, and my skin tingles at his soft words.

"I love you, too," I whisper as his arms swallow me in a tender embrace.

And I really mean it.

Releasing me and pulling away, he raises an eyebrow.

"Now, are you ready to go?"

I let out a massive sigh and nod. Here we go. Let the dread begin.

When we arrive at Shelby's gender reveal, I do a double-take, because it sure seems like we're pulling up on a frat party. Not that I have ever been to one. Community colleges don't have fraternities, and I wasn't exactly the type to party anyway.

But from the lame comedy shows Spencer watches, this seems to fit the bill. Women in ripped skinny jeans and crop tops mingle with dudes wearing backwards caps and sports jerseys. And everyone has a red plastic cup in hand.

I suddenly feel out of place in my flowy striped blouse and tan capris. I am clearly not showing enough skin for this crowd.

Spencer squeezes my hand as I push through the throng of bodies looking for a gift table. Instead, I find one lined with shooters of every type and a sign ordering us to "Take a shot, Cause I cannot."

Well, if she insists.

I drop the pastel yellow gift bag with my obligatory children's book and stuffed animal and scoop up a handful of tiny bottles. I hold one up to Spencer, but he shakes his head.

"You go ahead and cut loose tonight. I'll drive home."

"Suit yourself," I say, cracking the first one and downing the watermelon-flavored liquor.

I wince as the alcohol bites the back of my throat on the way down. Other than the occasional glass of wine or can of beer, I rarely touch alcohol and haven't been drunk since that one time in high school.

I hated how out of control it made me feel, and if memory serves, I was in absolute hell the following day. But tomorrow be damned! Right now, I welcome the numbness.

"Eeee!"

A girlish squeal breaks through the uproar of voices and music.

Shelby breaks through the cluster of people surrounding her and bounds up to me, grasping my arms. She's practically bouncing in place with uncontained enthusiasm.

"I'm so glad you came!" she shrieks with glee.

As if my attendance was optional.

"Of course," I say flatly.

I'm betting it's not socially acceptable to say, *"I'd rather be anywhere but here. I'm secretly green with envy that you're pregnant, while the baby I have been wanting for 5 years died last week."*

"The reveal is in 10 minutes, so don't go too far. Have fun!" she demands before stepping away to continue mingling.

I fight the urge to roll my eyes. I glance toward Spencer and see a look of disapproval briefly cross his face. He must have picked up on my icy demeanor.

He can take his disapproval and shove it.

I drown my frustration with another shooter — this time, cream tequila. I choke on the milky texture and sharp taste as my throat closes over the raging inferno it ignites on the way down. The alcohol hits me faster than I expect, but I don't care. Sputtering, I gasp for air, instinctively reaching for Spencer's arm.

Ever the hero, he produces a lukewarm bottle of water.

"Here, take a sip. You need to slow down."

Finally able to breathe again, I shoot him a glare.

"I'm fine!" I huff, pushing myself away from him and into the crowd.

Along the back wall, I find a poster board plastered with pink and blue sticky notes. Guests are lined up waiting to place their bets on whether Baby Peters will like pickups or makeup.

I could seriously hurl. How unbelievably tacky.

Cutting the line, I grab a pad of sticky notes and a Sharpie.

With zero thought, I begin scribbling fake names and sticking them willy-nilly to the board.

A murmur of displeasure rises from the people behind me. I barely notice.

Suddenly, I'm aware of someone gripping my elbow and carefully steering me away from the disgruntled crowd.

I'm just having some fun.

"You're having a little *too* much fun," Spencer chastises.

Wait, I said that out loud?

"Yes, Taylor, you said that out loud. You're drunk."

Okay, what is going on, and why does it feel like I'm walking on stilts? Suddenly feeling unsteady on my feet, I careen to the left, narrowly escaping a collision with the wall.

"Okay, party girl, time to go," Spencer hauls me to an upright position and guides me to the exit.

But we just got here. I dig my heels in.

"I'm fine, Spence." He stiffens at my slurred use of his nickname.

"We're going," he says with an edge to his voice.

Sensing his rising irritation, I attempt to stand up straight and glare him down. The room blurs as grief, rage, and 90-proof alcohol collide, sending me spinning off my axis.

"I don't need anyone to take care of me. And I don't need you!"

He visibly winces, and I realize I've shouted those words. Those in close proximity quiet their conversations and begin to blatantly stare.

"Taylor, let's talk about this later," he offers in a low tone, still trying to cajole me into stepping outside.

What was meant to pacify me just pisses me off more.

"Stop trying to protect me! Our baby is dead, Spencer. No

one can help me!"

It was as if someone turned the volume in the room down to mute. Everyone has ceased their interactions and is openly gawking. Tears prick my eyes as I see a horrified Shelby across the room. I can't face this anymore and bolt for the door.

Spencer trails behind me as I cross the parking lot toward his SUV.

The party continues without us, and minutes later, I hear a balloon pop and cries of "It's a girl!"

My gut aches with sudden nausea and anguish.

Finally catching up with me, Spencer grabs my arm and pulls me toward him. I force myself to look at his grief-stricken face, pushing down the remorse for my harsh words.

"You know it hurts me, too, that we lost our baby."

A fresh wave of anger rises.

"That's what you don't get, Spencer," I spit, "*We* didn't lose the baby. *I* did. Me."

I punctuate my words with a finger to his chest.

"I'm the one who failed. I lost the baby." I say, finally dissolving into tears.

He pulls me close, and for one blessed minute, I take comfort from his arms. But my alcohol-fueled anger kicks in again. I pull away and wordlessly climb into the car and slam the door.

For a beat, he just looks at me through the dusty window and looks about as lost as I feel.

Maybe now he'll understand.

Chapter 13

Shame follows me to work on Monday. I am not the girl who drinks too much and causes a public scene. I can't even remember the last time I got tipsy. And the only other time I've been rip-roaring drunk was in high school.

It was the three-year anniversary of my mom's death, and Spence and I had just started dating. After school, he drove me to a party in the middle of a cornfield where I experienced Fireball for the first and last time.

He had to carry me back to the truck after I made an ass of myself in front of his friends. I later tried unsuccessfully to seduce him and wound up hurling my guts out on the side of the road.

Instead, he took me back to his house and gave me a clean set of clothes before I snuck back home. Always the gentleman, always taking care of me. And this is how I treat him in return.

I'm jarred out of my thoughts as a pastel blue sticky note with the words "Seymour Leggs" scrawled across it thwacks against my computer monitor.

"What the hell, Taylor?"

I can't turn to face Shelby. I don't want to see the disapproval on her face or feel the cut of her wrath at me for single-handedly blowing up her gender reveal.

My alcohol-fueled frenzy was probably highly documented by her social media-crazed friends. I don't care to relive that moment, so I stayed off my phone all weekend.

"Taylor?"

She gives my chair a twist so I'm forced to face her. I slowly meet her gaze, only to find a hint of humor twinkling in her green eyes.

"You go all Britney Spears, but instead of shaving your head, you doodle fake names on Post-Its?" She arches an eyebrow in an attempt to be scolding, but I can sense her fighting back a smile.

I mumble an apology, but guilt chokes off my words.

"Damn, girl. Are you okay? I mean… The way you laid into Spencer. Whew." She blows out her breath.

"I'm sorry I caused a scene and humiliated you in front of your friends," I say, hanging my head.

Shelby lowers herself to my level.

"I don't care about those people, Tay. I care about *you*."

Her words rest heavy on me yet somehow lighten my leaden heart.

"Why didn't you tell me?" she probes.

"What? That I was so bitter envious of you for getting pregnant without even trying when I've been wanting a baby for years?"

I throw the words out there, expecting them to fester like a poison, but Shelby doesn't bat an eye. She nods at me expectingly.

"Cause that's an awful thing to say?"

"You know you can tell me anything, even if it's awful."

The lump in my throat expands, and I fight the prick of tears behind my eyes.

"Are you okay? How are things at home?" The empathy in her voice soothes me.

"Spencer hasn't spoken to me in days," I say.

"I'm sorry. If you need someone to talk to, I'm here."

Hearing a familiar voice enter the next cubicle, I groan. Jenna. If she witnessed my absolute meltdown, the entire office will know by lunch. The shame drains every ounce of blood from my face.

"Was Jenna…" I angle my head toward her desk, unable to get the question out.

Shelby sighs, "She showed up late, got hammered, and my cousin Eric drove her home."

Relieved, I let out a deep breath and give Shelby a weak smile. She squeezes my hand and turns, and heads back to her desk.

"And another thing," she glances back at me. "Next time, go with 'Hugh Jass'"

Her slow chuckle finally has me cracking a slight smile.

* * *

I don't feel like feeling. I lift the third powdered donut to my chapped lips and take a bite of the sugary confection.

The sweetness melts over my taste buds, and I close my eyes in enjoyment. I so rarely indulge myself this way, but hell with it. I wash it down with a swig of lemonade and wipe the sugar off on the front of my jeans.

It's been a week since my blowup at Shelby's party. Each night, Spencer comes home a little later than the night before, eats in silence, and goes straight to the bathroom to shower.

Outside of a few mumbled greetings, he has managed to avoid me at every turn. In the few brief moments I've caught his eye, I have seen the hurt etched into his expression.

I know I've done irreparable damage to us, and I don't know how to fix it. Part of me wants to reach out to him, but the louder voice in my head is still angry. I shouldn't feel guilty. *I'm* the one grieving.

As I polish off my pack of donuts, I hear his feet shuffling on the back step. He enters wordlessly and heads to the sink to scrub his grease-stained hands.

"Supper's on the stove," I murmur, gesturing to the half-eaten, lukewarm frozen pizza.

He nods and turns abruptly to throw a few slices on a plate. He then moves to the table and eats in silence.

"Okay then," I say casually and step out of the room.

He has clearly shut me out, and I hate how much that hurts. A random tear leaks from the corner of my eye, and I swipe it away miserably.

No. I'm done being sad. I'm angry.

Angry at the universe for taking away my chance at the only thing I ever wanted. Now, all I am left with is bitterness. It's not a fact I'm proud of, but a fact, nonetheless. I have always excelled at hiding my feelings under a warm smile to those who don't know me. I can cover my anger with sarcasm and humor, remaining in everyone's good graces.

But somehow, that control seems to be slipping.

If I've learned anything in life, it's that everyone eventually hurts you if you let them get close enough. I have learned to keep everyone at arm's length, and now that includes Spencer.

I have been searching for a safe place to vent, to cry, to

scream. But there is no such space for me. My life is not my own but a strange collage of everyone's expectations. Instead, I'm just going through the motions with no thoughts or feelings of my own.

My phone buzzes with an incoming call. When I see Leslie's name pop up, I send it to voicemail. I've dealt with enough today.

Moments later, I see a new voicemail notification. I really don't want to listen to whatever she has to say, but the curiosity gnaws at me.

"Taylor, have you dropped off the face of the earth? I have been trying to reach you for weeks. How can you ghost me in the middle of wedding planning? Peter's sister has been helping with the shower arrangements since you can't be bothered to text me back. But it's next Sunday, and I need you to be there. Please, sis? Call me."

I hear the desperation in her voice, and remorse squeezes my chest like a vice. Since the bachelorette party flop, I have completely bailed on her. Another confrontation today is going to end me. I'll fix this tomorrow.

* * *

Another mind-numbing week passes. Despite our conversation after the gender reveal, Shelby seems off. Like she's treading carefully around me because I'm liable to snap at any moment. I don't know, maybe it's all in my head. I'm good at reading between lines that don't exist.

I glance down at my smartwatch to check the time for the third time this morning: 10:01

Why do I keep feeling like I'm forgetting something?

After waking up around 8, I have been dragging my butt, just trying to find any sort of motivation today.

I took a 45-minute shower in steaming hot water, hoping to cleanse my soul of the darkness that has all but absorbed me. I dressed in sweats, which happened to be the last of the clean laundry.

Typically, Spencer would pick up the slack whenever I've been too ill, busy, or moody, but he's barely been here. His shifts at work continue to run late. Some days, I wouldn't even know he'd been home if not for the Spencer-sized warm spot in the mattress next to me each morning. Although he's supposed to be off on weekends, he's made himself scarce. Today, he woke up early, muttering something about helping a buddy overhaul an old truck, and has been gone all morning. It almost feels like he's making up excuses to not be around me.

Truthfully, I have been floundering since my outburst at Shelby's party. I have always known about Spencer's chronic avoidance issue, but this is the longest we've gone without mending fences.

I'm about to pick another fight just to get him to speak to me again. I can't handle the silence, not from him.

I groan as I shift my weight on the couch. My laptop is propped up beside me, streaming another dumb rom-com, when my phone buzzes.

Leslie: *"You really couldn't be bothered to show up?"*

Shit. Shit. Shit.

Leslie's bridal shower brunch. I completely forgot. I must be the worst sister in human history. My stomach lurches, and I race to the bathroom just in time for my breakfast of potato chips and marshmallows to splatter into the toilet bowl.

I sprawl out on the floor, stomach twisting with regret. There's nothing I can even say that could fix this. What excuse could I possibly come up with?

"Sorry, sis. I couldn't make it to your shower because I was too busy feeling sorry for myself. Maybe next time."

That would go over about as well as a bomb with my bridezilla baby sister.

I dig my fingers through my tangled hair and let out a low groan. Two small tears leak out of my eyes and trickle down to fall into my ears.

I'm a goddamn mess. I don't even know who I am anymore. I was always so put together, emotions firmly in check. Even on my worst days, I never came close to the train wreck I have become.

I drag myself to my feet and face my reflection in the mirror. I look like crap. Baggy eyes. Greasy hair. Splotchy cheeks.

I pinch the roll of flesh along my side. Yup, I've definitely put on a few more pounds. Feeling disgusted, I pull my phone out of my bathrobe pocket. My fingers itch to text Spencer — wherever he is.

I want to fix us because I am withering in his absence. Clearly, I was not meant to be left alone in the world.

What do I say?

I stare at his contact picture on my screen, a smiling photo of the two of us taken on a camping trip a few years ago. We had taken a break from trying to get pregnant and decided to vacation in the wild mountains of Montana for a week.

Smiling wistfully, I remember hiking backcountry trails, canoeing across the lake at our campsite, and attempting to fly fish in the alpine streams.

Spencer had taken about a million pictures of the trees,

wildlife, and me. Annoyed by my shutterbug's constant clicking, I sassed him about the lack of proof of his even being on the trip since his camera card only contained pictures of me.

He just smiled, flipped his camera around, and captured one single selfie. To this day, it is one of the few pictures we have together outside our wedding photos.

Whenever someone suggests we take a group picture, he always manages to disappear or have a ready excuse. Usually, it's a tired line about his fear of "breaking the camera" or something equally asinine.

I smile sadly at the photo until the phone screen goes black. I miss the people we were with on that trip. We were happy then, despite the infertility struggle. We still had hope that everything would work out. I'm not sure things were ever the same when we came back home to reality.

I wish I could go back to that place and tell us to never leave.

* * *

By some sheer willpower, I manage to drag myself to work on Monday, cringing at the fact that I'm running 15 minutes behind. Being late is not something I do, so I brace myself for the wrath of Sandra. I know I have not been showing up as my best self lately, as I have been quite frankly half-assing everything. I tiptoe past her office to see that the light is off and the door is closed. Luck is smiling on me today.

I continue toward my cubicle, and when I pull back my chair, a single cupcake is resting on my desk. Glancing around for the mysterious gift giver, I only see heads bent over keyboards.

Jenna is talking on the phone, and by the sounds of the

conversation, it's definitely not work-related.

I stifle an eye roll and sit down, casting a look toward Shelby's area. I don't recall her mentioning she was going to be out today. I wonder if she's secretly mad at me. Something doesn't feel right there. But maybe it's just me.

Logging into the computer, I set about my tasks for the day. Too many projects have been piling up while I've been wallowing.

I pull down some data sets and start compiling a couple of email campaign reports that Sandra asked for last week. I'm knee-deep in numbers when I hear a high-pitched shriek behind me.

I spin in my chair, recognizing Shelby's voice.

"Hey, birthday girl!"

I give her a blank stare.

"Don't tell me you forgot your own birthday!" She says in jest.

I glance at the calendar. Well, shit.

"Uh, yeah, I guess I kinda did," I mumble.

"Dang, you really are messed up," she teases.

She doesn't realize that she's spot on.

"So sorry, I wasn't here this morning. I had a last-minute doctor's appointment, but I left you a treat before I went in."

Ah. The cupcake was from her. Suddenly, I realized that it's late in the afternoon, and I worked through lunch. I also realize her cupcake was the only thing I've eaten today. As if on cue, my stomach decides to gurgle.

Shelby laughs at the sound.

"You got big plans tonight with Spencer?"

I shake my head sadly.

"Are you two *still* not talking?"

“Nope,” I say, giving the ‘p’ an extra pop.

I stare at my hands as if they hold some sort of answer to the world’s problems — or at least the problems in my marriage.

Shelby hmms, pondering my response.

“How did Leslie’s shower go? Stuffy, I imagine?”

Fresh guilt presses down on me.

“I didn’t go.”

“Seriously?” Shelby asks with a hint of concern in her voice.

I make eye contact with the carpet. “Yeah, um, I forgot that too.”

“You forgot your own sister’s bridal shower. And you’re the matron of honor?” Shelby says without accusation in her voice.

I say nothing. I already know what she must be thinking, and I can’t face her judgment. What kind of sister does that?

“I know I’ve made some jokes, but this is serious, Tay,” Shelby says.

Taking a seat on the edge of my desk, she palms her slightly rounded belly.

“I know life handed you a shit sandwich, but you need to face this and try to move past it. This isn’t healthy.”

A flash of anger heats my insides. What does Shelby know about what I’ve been through?

Whipping my eyes up to meet hers, I unleash my fury.

“Oh, I have to face this, Shelby?” My cheeks redden with my anger. “Does your dance club fling know that he’s going to be a father? Or have you not gotten around to facing that?”

The moment the words are out there, I want to claw them back. Shelby visibly flinches as if I just reached out and slapped her. Without a second glance, she drops off my desk and marches away. A gaping hole widens in my chest as I stare after her in utter disbelief at what I've just done.

I've just lashed out at the last person who was in my corner.

Chapter 14

Driving home from work usually lightens my mood, but today nothing can shake the sour feeling in my belly.

I have officially reached rock bottom. I thought there was no way I could claw my way back after my drunken antics at her party, but how can I come back from this?

Pulling into my driveway, I shift the car into park and rest my head against the steering wheel. The warm leather on my forehead does little to soothe the rising ache behind my eyes.

I groan audibly and wrench myself out of the car, toss my purse over my shoulder, and slowly walk down toward the mailbox.

Seeing the irises and phlox blooming along the sidewalk does nothing to lift my spirits as it typically would. I just feel lifeless inside.

Gathering the stack of bills, bank statements, and junk mail, I walk up to the front door, shuffling through each piece of mail with mild curiosity.

I fumble with my key in the lock, as a letter from the bank

catches my eye. With the door halfway open, I stop and tear the envelope open.

Enclosed is a brief thank you for opening a new account in the amount of $10,000. A new account? There must be some mistake.

I flip back to the mailing address and confirm it is indeed addressed to Spencer Swanson. My heart drops.

Where did he get that kind of money? What on earth could it be for?

My fingers tremble as I unlock my phone and pull up our bank account app. The total in our checking account looks right. So where did this sudden influx of cash come from, and how does he intend to use it?

Maybe he's leaving you.

The thought whispers in the back of my mind. God. What if he leaves me? My mind whirls with possibilities, and my heart digs itself deeper in the mire.

How do I keep from losing him? Maybe I already have.

I tap my toe repeatedly against the leg of the wooden coffee table, nervously awaiting Spencer's arrival from work. I try to shut down the rising panic in my head by shifting my focus to what I can see and feel in front of me.

I study the knots and grain of the hardwood floor as my hand gently brushes the soft microfiber finish on the couch. There's still a faint blood stain on the middle cushion despite Spencer's valiant effort to scrub it clean. The spot forever taunts me, reminding me of what I lost. Pushing it from my mind, I glance around the room. This once bright and cheery space is showing signs of age. The ceiling bears brown rings from water damage, the crown molding is pulling away from the wall in the far corner, and the sage green paint is chipped and faded.

We poured so much love into this old house when we moved in 10 years ago, but that love has slowly eroded. My heart aches at the thought of what time wears down and slowly destroys.

At last, I hear the shuffling of boots as he steps through the kitchen door. A lump forms in my throat, full of words I can't seem to pull up from my lungs.

He lifts his weary head in my direction as he crosses the floor, nods once, and ducks into the bathroom.

My chance to corner him and demand answers has passed for now. Maybe for the best. Time. I need time to clear my head and form my thoughts into words without losing this new fiery temper.

Ping!

A phone chime from the kitchen piques my curiosity.

Ambling toward the sound, I notice Spencer left his phone and wallet on the counter. From across the house, I hear the sound of the shower turning on.

I fiddle with my wedding ring, curiosity gnawing at me. I want so badly to know what is going on with him, but what if I don't want to know? What if it shatters everything?

Taking a deep breath, I give in to temptation. Snatching up the phone, I can see the new message flashing across the screen.

Ashley O'Neal: I am definitely interested. When can I come over?

I wince as if I've just been burned, and the phone drops from my hand and lands with a crack on the tile floor.

Suddenly, a conversation with Shelby the other day came to mind. I brushed off her probing questions about Spencer cheating at the time. But what if she was right?

It would explain everything — the late nights and never being home, the mysterious bank account, the fact that he can't even look at me anymore. Now this?

I can't give him the one thing he needs, and he turns to another. Part of me can't blame him, and the other part can't believe he could betray me like this. The rational side of my brain shuts down, and all that is left is fury. After all this time? How could he?

Marching toward the bathroom, I hear the water shutting off. I pull open the door, ready for war, but I pause as I see him toweling himself off, water droplets glistening along the bulk of his arms.

Despite my anger, my body betrays me, reacting to him the same way it did at 17. The once-sculpted muscles of his chest, toned from hours of football practice, have softened a bit with age. The sun-bleached hair from summers spent working outdoors has faded to a dull blonde after years of being covered by a welder's helmet. But despite all this evidence of time taking its toll, he is still as handsome as he ever was. The years have only made him more distinguished, from the grease-stained boy working on cars to the steady and hard-working man.

While time breaks most things down, it somehow builds people up. I push through the feelings of nostalgic desire and steel myself to face his betrayal.

"Who the hell is Ashley?" I snap

He gives me a puzzled look, and I continue.

"Are you cheating on me?"

Looking aghast, he finally speaks. "Of course not! Why would you think that?"

"Oh, I don't know, Spencer. Maybe the fact that you're never here. You're always 'working late.' Your shift ends at 6, and yet you don't roll in until after 10 sometimes. When you do decide to grace me with your presence, you can't be bothered to say two words to me."

My anger heightens. He looks like he wants to say something, but I keep going.

"And I know about your secret bank account. Ten grand, Spencer? Where did you get that kind of money? And what are you planning? Is this to fund your insane business idea or just to bankroll your new girlfriend?"

Even as I say it, the wild accusation burns across my tongue like poison. I know I'm jumping to conclusions, but I can't stop myself.

"I don't know what you're even talking about. Girlfriend? I don't even *know* an Ashley. And as I told you, I have been taking on extra hours." Spencer's irritation is evident in his tone, but I couldn't care less.

I thrust the phone into his hand with the incriminating message still blazing on the home screen.

"Really, Taylor?" His eyes narrow. "This lady is interested in the mountain bike I'm selling. If you'd opened the message, you would have seen that."

Despite being a bit deflated, I stand my ground. "Okay, but the mysterious bank account? You can't just explain that away? I'm not stupid, and I know something is going on!"

Spencer retreats to the bedroom and begins throwing on clothes.

"You can't keep avoiding me!" I yell.

"Isn't that what you want?" He suddenly shouts, taking me by surprise. "You don't want me to take care of you. You mock me for grieving for a baby that I also lost! Damnit, Taylor. It's not always about you!"

My lower lip quivers. Never once has this gentle man ever raised his voice to me. As if sensing my apprehension, he lowers his tone.

"I took on more work because I needed an escape. Cause I'm hurting too. Can't you see that?" I see the brokenness in his eye, but I stubbornly can't let this go.

"But what about the money, Spencer?" I snap.

Fresh anger flashes in his eyes as he throws his coat on and strides for the back door.

"Where are you going?!"

"I need some air," he mutters.

"Are you leaving me? Is that what the money is for?"

With one hand on the doorknob, he slowly turns back to me.

"If you really think so low of me after all this time together, I need to reconsider who I married. And if you must know, the money is from my 10-year bonus check. It's a Health Savings Account. I was hoping, when you were ready, we could use the funds for further treatment."

My jaw slackens, and I wish I could rewind the last few minutes and delete everything I just said. But I made my stance, and now I'm going to lose everything.

Pain etches hard lines around his eyes as he says the last part, "I love you, Taylor. I always will, but I don't know if I can do this anymore."

Without another word, he walks out and closes the door firmly behind him.

I physically feel the last of my anger melt from my body and puddle on the floor. I feel like a wrung-out washcloth that has been balled up and left to dry in a crumpled heap.

I can't even cry. I'm too numb. I thought I had already hit rock bottom, but I apparently dug myself in deeper. How could I have missed the mark? I can hardly even believe what I accused him of. I don't even know who I am anymore. I'm not this jealous, sniping person.

The familiar coat of self-pity drapes over my shoulders as I try to wrap my mind around life without Spencer. Sinking to the floor, I finally give myself over to the sobs ripping from my body.

Happy fucking birthday to me.

I don't even know how long I've been curled into the fetal position on the floor, but I can't go on like this. I need to get my shit together and convince him to stay. Yes. Maybe I can fix this. If I can just talk to him. Buoyed by a sense of hope, I reach for my phone, but before I can get it unlocked, it rings in my hand.

An unknown number flashes, and instead of ignoring, like usual, I take the call.

"Taylor Swanson?" a gruff male voice asks.

"Yes, this is her." My stomach knots with apprehension.

"Ma'am, I'm afraid there's been an accident. It's your husband."

Chapter 15

A slow and steady beeping echoes behind my closed eyes. Terror grips me as I realize I have dozed off, and I'm just now realizing where I am.

I wish this were all a bad dream, but as I lift my aching head from the edge of Spencer's hospital gurney, my stomach clenches.

His bruised and swollen face is barely visible beneath tightly wrapped bandages.

The drive to the hospital last night was a blur, and I only recall bits and pieces of the doctor's words amid the various tests and scans: "Broken femur. Hairline skull fracture. Monitoring brain activity."

After bouncing from the ER to a waiting area to the ICU, my nerves are still a jangled mess. Will Spencer wake up? And if he does, will he ever be the same?

"All we can do is wait and see. Brain injuries are tricky that way," the on-call nurse told me last night.

She had given me a sympathetic smile before taking his blood pressure and checking his IV line.

"He's young and strong, and his vitals are good." There was a hint of hope in her voice at that. Then she nodded once and pulled the door closed behind her, boxing me in with my fear.

Throughout all the chaos, I have lost track of time. I pull my cell phone from my purse, but the battery has gone dead overnight. From the low light glinting into the window, I can tell it is still early morning.

I groan as I make my way to the bathroom to splash some water on my face. My entire body hurts from sleeping with my face against the cool plastic railing of his hospital bed.

Feeling somewhat more alive, I drop back into my chair beside his bed, studying his still form. His leg has been stabilized, but with the swelling on his brain, it was too risky to take him to surgery last night. The doctor warned me that even if he recovers from his head injury, he may never walk the same again.

Apparently, he was T-boned at a red light just before midnight. I don't even know where he was going. I wonder about the condition of the other driver, the one who had too much to drink last night. Does he have a family, and are they in as much anguish as I am? The anger that has become so familiar to me lately is gone. I think I burned through the last of my rage last night. I should hate that young man for the consequences that my husband is paying, but I can't seem to summon the energy.

Cold fear is the only emotion I can register. I reach toward Spencer's battered but warm hand and take it in both of mine.

"Please." I whimper. "Please don't leave me."

If there is a God, then I need a miracle, and I need it fast.

Once a brain injury occurs, a ticking clock is set into motion.

He's been out for over 12 hours now. how long until they start asking questions that I don't have the answer to? I know Spencer didn't want to ever be hooked up to life support, but I can't be the one to let him go. Please, God, don't let it come to that.

Why couldn't it have been me? He didn't deserve this. I'd give anything to switch places with him.

"Taylor?" A roughened voice calls from the doorway.

I turn to the older man, expecting to see another doctor in a lab coat here to give me an update on Spencer's condition. Instead, I'm faced with a strange yet familiar face.

The man's once fair brown locks have faded to a steel grey, and his soft blue eyes are encased in wrinkles. My heart stutters for a moment.

"Dad?"

The man has aged considerably since that awkward Christmas morning 3 years ago. The day he thrust my mother's words upon me and sent me into a tailspin. Why is he here? The familiar resentment stirs within me.

"Teresa told me what happened," he says in explanation. Of course, Spencer's mom would cross the street to share the news. I think she knew how strained our relationship had gotten.

"You just missed her, she had a shift at the clinic," I say, flatly.

He nods and slowly limps his way into the room, leaning heavily on a wooden cane. I didn't realize he had difficulty walking. Perhaps Leslie had mentioned something offhandedly amid all her wedding planning chaos, but I hadn't been paying attention.

Guilt grips me once again. I haven't been focusing on anything but myself all these months — maybe even years.

As if sensing my distress, the feeble man I barely recognize steps toward me and rests a hand awkwardly on my back.

Despite the tension, I pull my knees to my chin and tears well up in my eyes for the first time since I got the call. Finally, I dissolve. As my shoulders shake from the sobs ripping from my chest, he remains stoic and silent.

Although he doesn't say a word, his presence brings a strange sense of comfort.

I finally bring myself to utter the single thought that has been in my head since I got that terrible phone call.

"What if he dies?"

I turn toward my father, who takes his time to answer.

"I know what it is like to lose a spouse," he says at last. "When your mother died, a part of me went with her."

He pauses again as if gathering his thoughts or maybe his courage.

"I was never a true father to you after that. You reminded me so much of her that it hurt to look at you."

Stunned, I reply, "Me? But Leslie has her looks."

"Yes, but you always had her free spirit. It kills me that her death stole that from you."

His age-stained hand trembles on the handle of his cane, his other rests like a brick upon my shoulder. It is as if the man is putting all of his energy into just staying upright. Despite the numerous chairs in the room, he chooses to stand — maybe because in this moment, I cannot.

I contemplate his words. My mother was a force of nature. She could tame the fiercest tantrum Leslie or I threw with a single arch of her brow and yet be laughing and chasing us around the yard a moment later. She had this uncanny way of always sensing what was on my mind, no matter how hard I tried to hold in my feelings.

I recall the advice she gave when I had my first crush in middle school. *"Taylor, there will be boys who come along and sweep you off your feet. But the one that continues to carry you despite all the bumps in the road of life is the one you should keep."*

God, she would have loved Spencer. He is everything a mother could ever hope for her daughter. And I didn't deserve either one of them.

"I don't ever remember being like her." I finally admit.

"Oh, but you were." He sighs sadly before dropping into the chair beside me. The eerily calm silence is only interrupted by the low beeping of medical equipment.

My father's presence dredges so much up from my childhood, while Spencer's very life seems to dangle by a thread. The collision of my past and my future leaves me reeling.

My voice is thick when I finally speak the words I've kept in for so long.

"I don't deserve him. I don't think I ever did." I pause, trying to gather myself, "The things I said to him…"

But my throat closes off before I can even complete the thought. I fight back tears as my father's weathered hand finds mine.

"Do you love him?"

I nod through my tears, "But it's not that simple."

"Love is love. The only complications are the ones we put there." He muses for a moment before continuing, "You know, out in the country, you find old farmhouses that have been abandoned and fallen into disrepair. Then some development company comes along and tears it down to make way for new homes and businesses. And just like that, a place once filled with so much life and love is erased completely. But with a lot of hard work, you can reset foundations, rebuild walls, and patch the roof. Sometimes those old houses wind up stronger than anything you can build brand new."

I snort. "You always said old houses were a waste of money with drafty windows and inefficient heating," I say, thinking back on the advice he gave us when we purchased our little old house.

He gives me a wink, "I may have gotten wiser through the years. Life teaches some hard lessons."

A dim smile tugs at the corners of my lips despite my current situation. It vanishes as quickly as it came while I ponder my father's words.

Is my house beyond repair? The memory of Spencer's final words echoes back to me.

I don't know if I can do this anymore.

"I'm not sure how to get through this. I don't know what I'll do if I lose him."

Losing him could come in different ways at this point. He could wake from his coma in a lessened capacity, or worse, he could regain his memory of that awful fight and outright walk away. I can't even stomach the idea of him dying. I'm not sure there's a way out of this that won't tear my heart to shreds.

"Faith." He whispers as if the word alone has magical powers.

I could hold onto hope, but it hasn't served me well thus far.

He pulls himself to his feet and shuffles toward the door, mumbling a goodbye and promising to check in on me again.

I feel comforted by that somehow. It's like there's a salve being placed over an old wound that can finally heal. As surprising and puzzling as his visit has been, I'm thankful that he came.

He pauses with his hand on the doorknob and looks back

at me with a gentle look in his eyes, "Forgiveness also goes a long way."

I slowly shake my head, "Spencer has done nothing that needs forgiveness."

He levels a knowing gaze at me. "Forgive your mother for leaving and forgive yourself for everything that's happened since."

* * *

Another day passes as if in slow motion.

Nurses bustle in and out, and doctors periodically provide updates, most of which make little sense to me. From what I have gathered, his condition remains unchanged. Spencer's mom has popped in and out sporadically. Her haggard face is a picture painted by years of sorrow. I don't think she ever recovered from the loss of her husband, and with her son's life in the balance, fresh fear shines in her eyes.

She rarely speaks while she's here — just holds his pale, scarred hands and stares at the angry bruises on his bandaged face. Her brown eyes are etched with terror, but I have yet to see her cry.

After several missed calls from work, I eventually gave notice of my two-week leave of absence. My fingers have itched to text Shelby about my predicament, but I still don't know where we stand. I'm not sure I know where I stand with anyone these days.

Leslie has texted that she heard the news. I know she wants to help, but I'm beyond help right now. She asked to come visit last night, but I told her I was too exhausted. The truth is that I can't bear the guilt of what I've done — to her or Spencer.

It's better to keep my distance.

Dad comes up to the hospital each morning promptly at 8:30, stays for an hour, and then returns home. Few words pass between us, but his presence has been oddly comforting — a reassurance that I'm not completely alone. Surprisingly enough, I've grown to look forward to his visits.

He's mentioned forgiveness several times now, and it has been tumbling around my head like towels in a dryer.

Maybe I have been angry with my mother all these years and, in some ways, sabotaging myself at every turn since then. Her life was cut short, and somehow, I stopped living too.

All my life I found myself as a boring, moody bookworm — a doormat who lived only to serve others and never herself. But my dad describes me as a vibrant and creative child. How could I have been both people?

Who even am I? And better yet: Who do I want to be?

The question I have been wrestling with reverberates back to me.

"Oh Spence." I murmur to my husband's still form. "I wish you could hear how sorry I am — how wrong I've been about everything. I still need you here."

The words seem to float in the empty room as my guilt wraps a clammy fist around my heart. I lower my weary head and fold my arms beneath it. I clutch Spencer's hand, cautious of the IV line placed near his wrist.

My eyes squeeze shut to contain my emotions.

"Taylor."

The soft word lingers in my mind as I flash back to a million memories of our lives together like the night of my high school graduation. He kidnapped me from my party and drove me out into the country. We'd been bickering for weeks on my future plans and whether or not we'd stay together. When an old Kenny Chesney song came on the radio, he pulled off into a corn field and asked me to dance. Out of the clear blue, he asked me to be his wife. I thought he had gone completely mad, but I was so in love I had to say yes.

"Baby."

Okay, I definitely heard something that time. Glancing up, I see Spencer's hand hovering near my face — reaching for me.

A dam bursts within me as tears and emotions flood me.

"Spencer!" I sputter. "Oh my God."

I press my face into that work-worn hand, and he gently lowers my head to his chest.

"You're okay." I sob over and over.

After seven terrifying days, Spencer is awake and alive. Thank God! Relief and gratitude melt away any remaining guilt as nurses rush into the room to check on him.

Right here in this moment, I know that my house can be rebuilt. As long as Spencer is here, we can fix this.

Chapter 16

"How are you holding up?"

The question jolts me from my staring contest with the vending machine.

I turn to see my dad adjusting his dark-rimmed glasses and flexing his fingers around the handle of his cane. He's wearing a cable knit sweater over a faded brown flannel shirt, and the denim of his jeans is looking a little faded. He looks like a retired farmer rather than the sharp-minded accountant I know him to be.

Above all else, he looks tired. Hell, I probably look worse. I glance down at my scuffed canvas shoes, rumpled shirt, and two-day-old sweatpants. I stifle the urge to sniff myself.

"I could use a shower," I shrug.

"I hear Spencer's awake." He says matter-of-factly.

I blow out a slow breath.

"Yeah, I didn't get much time with him last night before he fell back asleep. He's in surgery now."

I finally punch in my selection at the vending machine.

Picking up the chocolate bar from the dispenser, I walk toward the man. I sink into a cushy chair in the waiting area, and he takes a seat across from me.

"The doctors say it's normal. His brain has been through a lot of trauma, but he's still Spencer."

"And you two are going to be okay?"

That same question has been pestering me as well. I know in my heart of hearts that we are going to figure this out, but there's a lot of work to be done. I need to fix what I broke.

"Yeah, I think we will be. I just need to make a lot of things right."

He looks at me curiously, waiting for elaboration.

Sighing, I decide to break my silence.

"I had a miscarriage a few months ago."

I fight for control of my emotions, and I look to my dad, expecting sympathy. But instead, I see . . . understanding. Some hard knot of pain releases inside me, and the story spills out bit by bit. I find myself telling him how closed off I've been, my outburst at Shelby's party, missing the bridal shower, and even our knock-down, drag-out fight before Spencer's accident. A few tears slide down my cheeks as I finally meet his knowing gaze.

I'm not sure if I expect to see judgment cross his face or maybe just apathy, but I'm shocked when a slight smile pulls at his lips.

"You're more like your old man than you know," he says finally.

I scoff, "You've single-handedly wrecked every relationship in your life?"

"I came pretty close once."

He pauses before taking a deep breath.

"You had a brother," he says slowly.

"What?"

"You were only about two when Faith got pregnant with our second child. Around 20 weeks, she started having contractions and had to go into the hospital. He was born a few hours later, the tiniest little thing you ever saw."

He pauses to swipe a tear from his weathered face before continuing.

"Caleb lived for a few minutes, and then God called him home."

"Caleb?"

"That's the name your mom had her heart set on, and it died with him. Oh, we tried again, for years, but it seemed impossible to have another child after that loss. We finally gave up the notion, and your mom poured herself into you. If you were going to be her only child, she was determined to make your childhood perfect. My soul still ached from losing Caleb, but when your sister came along, a bit of that hope was restored."

My heart squeezes with empathy.

"It's all in your mother's journal. I knew you and Spencer were struggling to start a family. I thought that if you read about our struggles, it would give you some hope. But that didn't go as planned…" he trails off.

Guilt consumes me. I'd taken his heartfelt gift as an attack and shut him out as punishment.

"Anyway," he continues, "Those years were pretty bleak for me. I, too, shut myself away from the world because, somehow, there was safety in that box I carved out for myself. I did the same after Faith passed away. For so long, she was that string that pulled me from the darkness of my own making. Without her, I was lost. Genie helped me find myself again, but by then, I had put too much distance between us. I've spent too many years afraid to reach out, worried you wouldn't want to hear from an old man who failed you so miserably. I was ashamed, and I let that fear hold me back."

Suddenly, everything clicks. I see the man in an entirely different light. Dad disappearing into himself was a response to his trauma. He always seemed stuffy and aloof, like I was just an afterthought. I resented him for so long and eventually just avoided him altogether. He has just been a man ruled by fear. Yeah, that sounds familiar.

"So why are you here now?" I ask softly, genuinely wanting to know how he found the courage.

"When I got the news about Spencer's accident, I knew I had to come. No one should go through that alone. Even if you turned me away at the door, I had to come. And more importantly, I had to forgive myself. Losing a child or a spouse is something that never stops hurting. But your reaction to that pain doesn't have to define you. You can decide who you want to be and how you want to show up in the world. And it starts with acceptance."

I ponder his words carefully. Can I accept myself and push through my fears? Is it really okay to be vulnerable? All I've ever done is try to protect myself, worrying about what others might think about me, and catering to everyone else's needs. I'm not sure I know how to change, but I know what I can do right now.

"Dad, I'm sorry I shut you out. I was so lost at the time, the thought of reading Mom's words was just too painful."

He gives me a knowing look. We both have undergone our fair share of pain. Then something unexpected happens.

"I forgive you, Dad," I whisper.

He looks like he wants to speak, but a strangled sound comes out instead. I lean over and rest my head on his shoulder. Looking up, I see another tear roll silently down his face.

* * *

The ex-con is on the run, and Detective Norris is closing in. I'm minutes from discovering who killed Mary Moore, and then my phone rings.

I reluctantly tear myself away from the murder mystery I've been engrossed in for the last week since Spencer woke up.

Ugh. It's Sandra.

I've been dodging her calls for the last two weeks. I can't bring myself to answer. I already know what she's going to say. My PTO is dwindling, and her KPIs won't track themselves. I just cannot bring myself back into that world right now.

My relationship with my best friend and cubicle mate is still on shaky ground, and the thought of analyzing data points on spreadsheets and creating reports has me feeling ill.

But I can't put this off anymore. I have to face this head-on. Gritting my teeth, I swipe my finger across the screen to answer.

Immediately, her shrill voice comes on, and I resist the urge to pull the phone away from my ear.

"Swanson! I have been trying to reach you for days. I need you back in the office today!"

"Sandra," I enunciate slowly and patiently, "I told you that I had a family emergency and needed to take a leave of absence."

She continues as if she didn't even hear me.

"I must say, your behavior as of late has been most unprofessional! We have an emergency with our latest email campaign. Our emails are being blocked, and we need you to fix it before our monthly report to corporate."

I hear the panic in her tone, and there are so many things I'd like to say. I've been trying to warn her for months that our email reputation was at stake. If her boss finds out that our domain has been blacklisted, her Chief Marketing Officer promotion will be off the table. Someone has been purchasing bad data right under her nose. I knew eventually it would send a big red flag to the Internet Service Provider, who would shut down our domain.

"Swanson, are you even listening to me?"

"Taylor," I correct her.

"Excuse me?" her startled tone sounds in my ear.

"My name is Taylor. You seem to keep forgetting that" I say calmly, "This isn't a college football team."

I can hear her sputter on her end of the call. No one ever stands up to her, and I've done it twice now. Shelby is the only other person in the office who doesn't cave to her every demand and wilt in her presence.

"I really hate to do this, *Swanson*." She bites back, "But I don't think it's in the company's best interest for you to continue working with us. Please clean out your desk by Friday."

My throat closes for a second. I shouldn't be surprised. Frankly, I'm shocked she didn't fire my ass the day I walked out of the office. My stay of execution was likely because, without my reports, she is dead in the water.

My flippancy and absence have proved too much for poor Sandra. So be it.

"Okay, Sandra." I say, coolly, "Please cut my severance check and have it ready then."

She begins to backpedal at that. Apparently, she expected me to fight or beg for my job.

"Um. Wait. We can probably work something out. If you just come into the office today, we can work through this… situation."

"You know, Sandra? I think you're right. I think it *is* in everyone's best interest if we part ways here. You have everything well at hand, and right now, I need to be with my husband."

I want to add, "Maybe you'd understand that if you weren't such an ass," but I refrain from saying anything childish.

Without waiting for a response, I end the call and let out a heavy sigh.

Yes, financially, this is going to suck, but I am bigger than that job. The money was good, but there was zero joy. Being in the place was like being sucked into poisonous quicksand. Always worried about meeting her insane deadlines, putting up with her abuse, and just the numbness of the job itself.

I may be good at crunching numbers, but not feeling any connection at all to the work is killing my soul. I'm surprised how relieved I feel right now.

For the first time ever, I have no idea where I'm headed, and I'm actually okay with that. All that matters is that I'm here with Spencer at my side, and he's going to get better.

I squeeze his hand to reassure myself of that.

"Hey," he says, lazily opening his eyes.

"Shoot, I'm sorry. I didn't mean to wake you."

"It's okay," he says, scrubbing a hand over his face before meeting my gaze. "Are you okay, though?"

"Well, I just got fired." I say frankly, "Or maybe I quit? I'm not sure which."

Spencer's jaw goes slack. "So, why do you look so calm? The Taylor I know would be hyperventilating right now."

I grin. "The Taylor you knew cared too much about what other people thought of her. To be honest with you, I fucking hated that job."

The admission is liberating. Spencer looks at me thoughtfully as I blurt out everything I've held back.

"For so long, I've been more worried about outward appearances and couldn't let anyone know how damaged I was inside. I kept everyone at arm's length, even you, because I thought no one could possibly understand the grief I've carried since my mom died. I thought having a baby would solve everything. I would have a connection to her, and our relationship would be saved. But then all these years of trying and failing to get pregnant…I've felt like such a disappointment. You wanted to be a dad, and I couldn't give that to you. Losing the baby almost ended me. But I couldn't see that you were hurting too. Instead, I lashed out and made things so much worse. You never deserved that. I'm sorry."

For a minute, he doesn't say anything, and my heartbeat quickens. What if I'm beyond forgiveness? What if this is only a temporary truce until he gets better, and then we go our separate ways? His words from the night of the accident taunt me.

"I don't know if I can do this anymore."

"This mess isn't entirely your fault," Spencer says, releasing a long breath.

I frown as he continues. "I've been going to the bar," he admits slowly, "At first it was just the one time to celebrate my 10-year anniversary at the plant. We were barely speaking at the time, and it felt good to get out of the depressing house, be around the guys, and have a few beers. It made me forget all our problems, at least for a few hours. So, I went again the following Friday and then the next. I started picking up as many extra shifts as I could, and when I got off early, I went to the bar. I didn't always drink. Sometimes I just sat and listened to the jukebox. Anything to avoid coming home and having another confrontation."

I cast my eyes to the floor. How did we wind up like this?

"I'm sorry you felt like you couldn't be around me," I say finally.

"No," he says, "I didn't know how to fix you when I was broken inside as well, so I just stopped trying."

A few weeks ago, this remark would have set me off, casting blame instead of understanding.

He squeezes my hand gently as he continues. "Taylor, you could never disappoint me. As much as I want to be a dad, I want to be your husband more. If we never have children, I'll still die a happy man, knowing I was loved by you."

The permanent weight on my soul lifts, and all the guilt I've carried begins to melt away. "You don't know how much I needed to hear you say that."

"I love you, Taylor. I won't give up on you. We can work through this. Together."

I smile as the last piece of frost melts off my frigid heart.

Chapter 17

Dread creeps up my spine. I stand on the pavement, staring up at the dark building before me. I've walked this sidewalk a thousand times in the past decade, swiping my badge at the door and taking the elevator to the 3rd floor. I never thought I'd see the day I wasn't clocking in and sitting down in my cubicle in the northwest corner next to my work wife and partner in crime.

I smile sadly as I think through everything Shelby and I have been through all these years. Interns that came and went, managers that moved through the ranks, and those that flamed out. We suffered through the server crash of 2020, in which we lost all our files and templates and had to start from scratch.

I guess in the end, none of it mattered because our relationship wasn't strong enough to endure everything I put her through. I can't prolong the inevitable. Squaring my shoulders and taking a deep breath, I walk through the double doors for the last time.

A second later, the elevator dings, and I begin making my

walk of shame through the marketing department.

Is everyone suddenly staring at me? I swear I can feel the gaze of curious eyes. But when I look around, everyone has their head down, typing or making phone calls. It's all in my head. Great. Now I'm losing my mind. I swallow the knot in my throat and continue on, noticing that Shelby's not here today. That's almost a relief.

Plopping down at my desk, I begin emptying years' worth of crap from my desk. I sort through the papers in my desk drawers, tossing irrelevant pages and organizing notes for my future replacement. I collect a few personal effects and drop them into a small box. A few family photos, a coffee cup, a fake succulent, and a few random office supplies I purchased. It's precious little to show for ten years.

Unease grips my stomach as I gather my things and head for the exit. I discreetly stop at Jenna's desk against my better judgment.

"Is Shelby out sick today?" I whisper, curiosity getting the best of me.

Jenna refuses to meet my eye.

"No, she's not here anymore."

"Miss Peters has been terminated for failing to adhere to company policy and our code of ethics," Sandra's voice sounds behind me.

What?

How could this happen? I whip around to face the she-devil.

"While you were *out*," she emphasizes, "It was discovered that she's been purchasing client lists and sending emails to prospects without their consent. Several users filed complaints, and we are being fined. Jenna pulled the login reports and saw the contact upload was done under her username."

I turn back to Jenna. "That's awfully funny, considering Shelby didn't even have permission in the email platform to upload contacts. That is an admin function."

I stare pointedly at her. For a second, I think I see a bit of shame cloud Jenna's eyes, but it vanishes into one of victory. They planned this. Sandra knew she was caught when I found the discrepancy in the report. Shelby was just the fall guy, and Jenna was more than happy to stab her friend in the back to get ahead. She didn't just lose her job; she lost her future. And now with a baby to support? A rock forms in my gut.

"You do realize that you could have IT scrub her computer to see if she truly performed that upload, or if it happened to be your little protégé here." I motion in Jenna's direction. "But my guess is that you honestly don't care. With Shelby out of the picture, no one will come looking at you. Plus, you don't have to pay for maternity leave. How convenient!"

Sanda just gawks, slack-jawed.

I give Jenna a final glance. "And congratulations on your promotion, Jenna. I hope it was worth it. I'm done with this place."

If this were a movie, there would be people standing and clapping as I make my grand departure instead of the mundane clacking of fingers on keys and ringing phones. No heroic send-off for me. So be it.

* * *

On a blistering hot mid-June afternoon after more than a month confined to a hospital bed, Spencer is finally able to come home.

The air conditioning unit hadn't been turned on all summer, making the house stifling. By the time I maneuver his wheelchair up the porch steps and through the front door, a bead of sweat rolls down my back.

"Home sweet home," I say with a laugh, as I plop into his easy chair.

"It feels so good to be back." Spencer shoots me a tired smile. I can tell the effort to get from the car to the chair wore him out.

"How about I get this A/C cranked, make us a quick supper, and then we can turn in early?"

Spencer sighs. "That sounds like a dream."

Two hours and a frozen pizza later, I help Spencer undress and get ready for bed. He falls asleep a second after his head hits the pillow, but I'm still restless.

I can't stop thinking about my mom's journal and the story of the brother I never knew. Rising from my side of the bed, I wander into the living room, pluck the book off my shelf, and drop into my window seat.

I open the worn cover and flip to the entries my father referenced.

September 26, 1996

My heart is gone.

At 6:00 this morning I woke up with strong Braxton Hicks contractions. I brushed it off until around 9:00 when I called my doctor. She suggested I come into the clinic to get checked out. I didn't want to worry Bradley, so I didn't call him at work. I was so sure it was nothing. But they couldn't slow down my contractions, and before noon, my little boy had arrived.

He took one gasping breath — his first and his last. Within a minute, he had died in my arms. I held him and cried until Bradley arrived from work, and the nurses took him away from me.

He didn't even get a birth certificate, but I named him Caleb Allen. I pray that he finds peace and that I find the strength to heal.

September 27, 1996

I was released from the hospital this morning. It feels so wrong to go home empty-handed. All the dreams I had of Taylor playing with her new sibling have burned to ash. I feel so hollow inside.

But being with her today has helped ease the pain in my heart. I did my best to explain the situation. She looked at me curiously and asked, "You miss your baby, mommy?" It almost killed me. I tried telling her that I missed him very much, but he went home to be with Jesus. Now she's toddling around the house, babbling about her baby brother in heaven. Her sweet innocence breaks my heart and heals it simultaneously.

My sweet Taylor is my whole world now. Somehow, the three of us will get through this pain together.

***

The nightmare returned last night. The bone-chilling fear and shrill pierce of screams bled into a hazy memory. It was me standing at the foot of her deathbed, too terrified to hold her hand or embrace her cancer-ridden body. My father's arms came around me, but I fought him off. That single memory became so warped that it haunted my dreams for so long.

Eventually, the scene shifted to a stone cottage nestled in a peaceful forest. An older woman with grey-streaked hair was standing on the stoop next to a young man with a dimpled smile and soft brown hair.

A tiny cherub-like child dashed out of the woods toward

them. "Faith!" the two adults exclaimed, "Welcome home!"

I awoke with tears streaming down my face and a singular knowledge in my heart. My lost baby made it to a better place. And she's not there alone.

Dim light filters in through the gap in the blackout curtains. Emerging from the covers, I cross the room and pull the heavy drapes aside. The sun is still low on the horizon.

Two squirrels chase each other around and around the base of the oak tree until they disappear into the upper branches. It's almost as peaceful as the dream that woke me.

I ponder the deeper meaning. Not only does it give me peace to believe my daughter is somewhere safe, possibly alongside her uncle and grandmother, but also, I think it is about accepting myself and all of the trauma I have gone through.

But there's one last thing to do.

Tiptoeing back to the bed, I check on Spencer. He's still sleeping soundly after his first night in his own bed. I place my hand gently against his face, and my heart clenches when I think of how close I came to losing him.

Dropping a kiss on his forehead, I turn and quietly leave the room. I make a right at the end of the hall and stop before the spare bedroom. Heaving a deep sigh, I turn the knob and step into the would-be nursery.

I've avoided this for too long. The last time I was in this room was the day I initially thought I lost the baby. In my pain, I hid everything out of sight and left this room as bare and empty as my heart.

Walking toward the closet, I slowly begin unpacking all of the items I purchased for my Faith. I start to organize piles of items I can donate and ones I want to save. Just because.

The familiar sting of pain hits as I imagine what my little one would have looked like in each outfit. How they might have played with the rattles and teethers. Would my baby have had Spencer's icy blue eyes or my dull blonde hair? I'll never know.

At last, I came across that carved wooden box. The things I use to hurt myself. A sad smile crosses my face. What an unfortunate way to look at it.

Opening the box, I pull out the tiny, crocheted booties. I clutch them to my chest, remembering the day my stepmother gifted them to me. I should finally take the chance to get to know her.

Lifting up the next item, my mother's silver cross pendant, I smile. I remember the way the sun always caught the chain, making it glitter like tiny diamonds. Pulling aside my hair, I wrap it around my neck and fasten the clasp. This is where it's always belonged.

My hands tremble as I reach for the newspaper clipping. I have not unfolded it in years, and the paper has yellowed with age. Taking a fortifying breath, I open it and read.

Faith Marie (Kilgore) Wells, aged 33, passed away peacefully on January 7, 2007, at her home in Oak Hills, Nebraska, after a lengthy battle with breast cancer. She was born on December 23, 1974, in Eve Lake, Illinois, to Gerald and Susan Kilgore.

Faith was a history major at Harmon University and spent a year studying abroad in Edinburgh, Scotland. While there, she fell in love with her Celtic ancestry and even picked up some Gaelic phrases.

A gentle soul and a free spirit, she spent some time traveling the country after college when she met Bradley Wells.

Faith and Bradley were joined in marriage a year later in 1991. Together, they were blessed with two children, Taylor Evelyn and Leslie Iris.

She worked at the Oak Hills Library and Sullivan's Art Gallery for many years. In her spare time, she volunteered for her children's school functions and various community and church events.

She was preceded in death by her parents. Left to mourn her loss are her daughters, husband, and a sister, Evelyn Walters.

Oh, how I miss her. Folding the paper back up, I set it gently back in the box.

Satisfied with my work, I stand to leave the room. But something catches my eye. Shoved in the furthest corner of the closet is an unopened Amazon box. Curious, I pull it out and rip off the packing tape. Inside, on a bed of foam, lies the replica derby car I had commissioned for Spencer's birthday.

Guilt hits me when I remember all the plans I had for his 30th birthday and how everything fell apart. He never even got to celebrate. He was too busy trying to fix me. I can't believe how badly I treated him. I don't even know why he's with me. He deserves so much better.

No. Wallowing in self-pity is what got me into this mess. If I want to be better, I can't go there. I won't go there. All I can do is focus on making things better today instead of wasting time worrying over the mistakes of yesterday.

With the car in hand, I walk back to the bedroom, where Spencer is just beginning to stir. I quickly ready his pain meds and a glass of water and set them on the nightstand.

"Morning," he mumbles drowsily.

"Hey," I say, hiding the car behind my back. "How are you

feeling?"

He grimaces, "Like a train hit me… twice."

He swallows down the capsules and takes a huge gulp of water, screwing up his face. I smirk, remembering how much he hates taking pills.

Noticing my suspicious demeanor, he cocks an eyebrow at me.

"Whatcha got there?"

"Who? Me? Nothing." I say trying to be cheeky.

Spencer grins at me, not buying it one bit.

"Out with it."

"Oh, this?" I say, producing the car, "Just a belated birthday gift."

Spencer lets out a low gasp. "Holy crow! It's Donna Sue!"

"Do you like it?"

"I love it! Where'd you get this? It's so detailed. The bumper is even crooked after that hard hit I took at the Bracken Ridge Derby!"

"Spence?" I say, interrupting his nostalgic moment.

"Hmm?"

I pause, gathering the right words in my head.

"I promise you that things are going to be better. *I'm* going to be better. Not just for us, but for myself. I spent too many years broken because of all the things that were out of my control. My mom's death, our struggles to have a baby, and now the miscarriage. I used that pain as a crutch and a weapon."

Spencer solemnly nods, taking one of my hands and tracing small circles on the back.

"And." I say with finality, "I'm going to be there every step of the way in your recovery. And maybe once things settle down and you're back on your feet, we can start trying again."

We deserve a fresh start, and I owe it to myself to find who I really am. A part of that means not giving up on my dream of becoming a mom.

Chapter 18

A few weeks after Spencer's return home, I decide to visit my dad. I had grown to miss his weekly chats in the hospital, and I figured a trip home was many years overdue.

Driving through the country always seems to settle my nerves. It never fails to bring peace of mind. Perhaps the fields of alfalfa bring back memories of my youth. Driving around at night in Spencer's old Dodge, singing every 90s country song that came through the radio static.

Spence always said I had the soulful voice of Trisha Yearwood. I remember rolling my eyes once, asking if that meant he was Garth Brooks. He then proceeded to belt out "Friends in Low Places" in an exaggerated drawl that sounded more like a tomcat than Garth.

We were so young. So carefree. We had the entire world ahead of us. I smile wistfully, thinking of those days as I turn off the highway into Oak Hills, population 408.

It's only been a few years, but it feels like decades. Despite only living an hour away, I have made a point to avoid our hometown. Spencer came back to help his mom move some things into storage a few years back, and I reluctantly came along.

I stood there across the street from the little house I grew up in, but I couldn't make myself walk over and knock on the door. I felt like an outsider, like I didn't belong.

Now, I can feel those same pesky feelings rising, and I force them down as I pull up into the drive. The tall spruce trees now tower far over the roofline of the small ranch house. The once bright white vinyl siding has yellowed with age, and the wide front porch is in desperate need of a fresh coat of stain.

But despite the signs of age, the home looks well-loved. The landscaping along the sidewalk is adorned with ornamental shrubs and cute little garden signs. There's a floral wreath on the front door and a checkered welcome mat.

I push aside my unease and step up to rap on the door, but before I'm able to knock, it swings open.

There stands Genie. Her once auburn hair is now completely white. But the same kindness shines in her eyes amid her gracefully aged face.

"Taylor? What brings you here, dear?" she says with a surprised smile.

"I was hoping to talk with my dad a bit. Is he here?"

"No, I'm afraid he's next door, chatting with Chip. You know how old men can gab," she says, inclining her head toward the tan house across the fence.

I faintly remember Dad being friendly with Chip Baxter. Back then, the grey-haired neighbor seemed decades older than my dad. Now, I guess they're both old men. Funny how time changes your perspective.

Taking my thoughtfulness for disappointment, Genie offers

an invitation.

"Why don't you come in, dear? I just made a fresh pot of coffee if you're interested."

"Sure," I say, stepping through the door of my childhood home.

The living room is much the same, yet somehow entirely different. The drab grey carpet has been replaced with laminate plank flooring, and the old boxy entertainment center is now a flatscreen on the wall.

But my grandpa's cane rocker is still in the corner, and the plant stand along the front window is still loaded with African violets and geraniums. My mother's white ceramic cat sits between the pots as if guarding over them.

Genie leads me into the dining room-turned breakfast nook adjacent to the kitchen. It feels so much larger than the cramped room I remember as a child, but removing the table and adding bench seating elevated the small space.

"Oh yes, I suppose things do look a bit different." Genie says, noticing my obvious gawking, "I forgot that it's been a while since you've been here."

I wince internally at the mention of my absence. She pauses as if realizing my sudden guilt and then continues in her conversational tone.

"With just the two of us, we didn't need that big old table."

She makes her way into the kitchen and pulls down two cups from some pegs by the coffee pot.

"Cream and sugar?" she asks softly.

"No, thank you."

"Ahh, just like your father. The blacker the better, he always says. Well, you'll love this extra dark roast."

She hands me a cup, and I take a careful sip. I tend to

be particular about my coffee, but I don't want to hurt her feelings. Surprisingly, though, it's delightful. Strong, smooth, and almost nutty.

"Mm, this is perfect. Really good flavor."

"It's some German blend. I can't pronounce the name," she chuckles. "Brad's got this subscription that sends him new flavors every month. I need at least a half bottle of creamer to get through a cup of this."

I smile down at the vastly different hues of our coffee.

"So why are you here after all this time?" she asks bluntly.

Setting my cup down on the small table, I meet her curious eye.

"Maybe I'm not even sure," I chuckle in spite of myself. "I'm still trying to figure things out, but Dad was there for me when I really needed someone."

"I remember the night of Spencer's accident." She muses softly. "Brad woke up with a horrible nightmare. He never said what it was about, but he felt it was a bad omen. He just kept muttering, 'Taylor needs me.' I had no idea what he was rambling on about. I thought he was half mad."

Her revelation shakes me to my core. How did Dad know?

"About 8 the next morning, Teresa knocked on the door and gave us the news. That poor woman." Genie shakes her head sadly.

I nod in understanding. Teresa Swanson looks like a woman twice her age. Grief has swallowed her alive all these years. I can sympathize with that.

"I want you to know," Genie says, looking at me in earnest, "I wanted to be there at the hospital, but Brad thought it best to go alone, given your history."

I offer her a small smile. "I still can't wrap my head around how he knew something was wrong."

She levels a wise look in my direction.

"Maybe *someone* was telling him at that moment that you needed him. Maybe you were never alone."

The air in the room feels thick as my feelings begin rising in my chest.

"Well," Genie says suddenly, slapping her hands on the table. "If you're all finished here, I have some irises to plant. What do you say we get our hands dirty?"

I follow her out the mudroom door. She hands me a bucket full of freshly dug iris shoots, a blue-handled trowel, and an extra pair of gardening gloves.

The backyard is far different from what I remember. My mother always kept perfectly groomed flower beds and landscaping, but in her absence, everything grew to a tangle of weeds and thistles. Under Genie's loving care, the order has been restored.

"Wow, this is beautiful. You've done a lot of work back here," I say in awe.

"Well, it had good bones. I just brought it back to life."

She leads me to the silver maple tree, where she has laid out a garden bed encircling the base of the tree. Landscape blocks form a barrier between the brightly colored blooms and the rest of the lawn. We begin laying out each plant 5 inches apart around the tree, and then set about digging each one into the ground.

We work silently for a few minutes, taking in the warm summer day. Birds sing to each other as the sun shines down through the leaves. Although I've always enjoyed flowers, I've never taken the opportunity to put trowel to dirt before. The tulips that pop up every spring by our mailbox were planted by the previous owner, along with the creeping phlox and irises along the walkway.

"Genie," I break the companionable silence.

She hmms, but doesn't look up from her digging.

"I'm sorry I never took the time to get to know you. And that I put so much distance between myself and Dad."

She looks up at me. "Oh dear, you were still grieving for your mom. We all understood that."

"But holding onto that pain kept me from having a relationship with you both all these years. I can't get that time back."

"Never waste your time wishing things could have been different. Guilt won't get you anywhere. You can realize your regrets and move on."

I nod, taking in her wisdom.

"But," she says, "I accept your apology. And you're always welcome at my table — and in my garden."

***

Driving back to the city, I reflect on my homecoming. After an hour in the flower bed, my father returned, and we talked until mid-morning when I had to head back to the city. I got what I came for — some genuine human interaction and a basket of home-baked goodness.

As I cut through the downtown area, I cringe as I pass the Apex Financial Solutions building. Somewhere up on the third floor, Jenna is probably celebrating her traitorous win, and Sandra is intimidating my replacement. I wonder if she will claw her way to her promotion, or if her dirty secrets will be her downfall. It's hard not to be curious about the company I dedicated my life to, but I don't miss the hell I went through.

I'm much happier on the outside.

Turning down a side street, I pull up in front of the physical therapy clinic. Lingering joy fills my heart when I push through the glass front doors to find my husband waiting for me in the lobby.

"Where've you been?" he says grumpily.

I stop short and frown at him, "I thought therapy ended at 11?"

"Ya," he barks.

Glancing at my watch, I see it's 11:08.

Okay then. I take it that this session did not go well.

"Well, let's get you home." I grab the handles of his wheelchair and propel him toward the door.

"I can do it myself!" he says, swatting my hands away and wheeling himself outside.

I know being laid up must be hard for a man like him. He's not used to being cared for, and he's been cooped up for far too long. I just need to be patient through his recovery.

At the curb, I help him out of his chair and into the passenger seat despite his grumblings and protests. Once he's situated, I struggle with the wheelchair, trying to figure out how to collapse it before shoving it into the trunk.

Thankfully, he's silent as I begin driving us back to the house, although I notice his jaw is clenched tight.

There's a storm brewing, and I try to break through the clouds. "Do you want to hit up a drive-thru on the way home?"

"No."

Got it. I take a deep breath and try to hold back the snarky comment that's about to fly out of my mouth. It's just the pain talking, I keep reminding myself.

At the house, he's still impatient and snappy as I get him out of the car. After a lot of effort, I manage to get his wheelchair up the two steps and through the front door. He wheels himself in front of the living room TV and turns on a baseball game.

Wordlessly, I begin assembling ham sandwiches for lunch. I make him a plate with some sliced strawberries and a handful of chips.

I walk into the living room and lean over to leave his plate on the coffee table.

"I don't want that!" Spencer roars.

In one rapid motion, he swings at me, swiping the plate from my hand. I faintly register a shattering sound. Pure, cold dread fills me. As I come out of my stunned stupor, I feel the pain licking my fingers from where his hand connected with mine. I see the glass shards and food scattered across the floor.

Still stunned, I look up to see the rage on his face slowly begin to melt into horror. As if he can't believe what he's done. Neither can I.

My eyes sting as I sprint from the room.

* * *

I hear a soft thump against the bedroom door. I set aside the leather-bound journal I have been heavily invested in ever since the accident. Somehow, I have found comfort in reading my mother's story.

Hearing the thump again, I glance up in time to see Spencer fumbling to swing the door open ahead of his chair.

I drop my gaze to the floor, unsure of what to say after his violent outburst.

"Taylor," he says gently.

I refuse to look at him.

"I-I don't know what came over me," he stutters. "I just felt...out of control."

He wheels himself closer, "Baby, please. I didn't mean to hurt you."

My feelings jangle inside. The realistic side of me knows this is likely a side effect of his pain medication, but the emotional side just can't come to terms with the fact that he swung at me. He. Hit. Me.

My gentle giant. My sweet, supportive Spencer. He would never do this to me. Maybe my house isn't on such unshakable ground.

Did I do something to deserve this?

No. I may have made my mistakes in the past, but this was unwarranted.

Spencer reaches out and grasps my hands in desperation.

"I'm so sorry." His voice is choked with emotion.

I finally meet his eyes, and I see the stark fear in his icy eyes. I'm not sure if the terror is because of what he's done, or of losing me.

"I know," I finally say. That much I know is true.

That cracked his resolve. He buries his face in my lap. I rest my hands on the back of his head, feeling the soft strands of his golden blonde hair.

I guess this year has brought both of us to our knees in more ways than one. If we can survive this, we can survive anything.

Pulling away, he reaches for my face.

"I'm done taking the meds," he vows adamantly.

"But you're still in pain," I protest, "Maybe we can talk to the doctor about adjusting your dosage or finding an alternative."

"No," he says, "I won't take that risk. I've read all the hospital pamphlets about addiction. I've been on them too long. It ends now."

I nod in understanding, but my head is reeling. How are we going to manage this?

"I know it's going to be hard, and I know I'm going to have to lean on you a lot. But we can get through this, okay?" he looks at me pleadingly, "Please don't give up on me."

"I'm right here." I stroke my thumb along his jawline. "I'm not going anywhere."

"That's just it. Until I *literally* get back on my feet, I think we're going to need some extra help around here."

Pondering his words and our current financial predicament, stress eats away at me.

"How would we afford a home health nurse? I'm pretty sure your insurance is tapped out at the moment."

"My mom was a nurse for years. I can ask her to swing by a few times a week to give you a break while you are looking for a job. With any luck, I'll be able to start using a walker or crutches in a few weeks."

I let out a sigh and try to put thoughts of money out of my mind.

Spencer launches into the details of his physical therapy plan and his countless weight-bearing exercises.

"If I keep to my PT three times a week and work on my upper body muscle strength, they think I can be walking with a cane by the end of the summer and return to light duty work by Thanksgiving."

Thankfully, disability should cover most of his income in the meantime, but the urgency for me to seek employment is rising.

Sandra's fear of exposure prompted her to write a hefty severance check in exchange for my silence. But that money will only get us so far when it comes to paying Spencer's rising medical bills. I want to text Shelby to make sure she's found a safe place to land, but I don't know what to say.

As for Spencer and me, we'll figure this out together. I know what happened wasn't the real him, but I can't forget it either. We both need time to heal.

***

The cursor blinks over and over, reminding me that I have yet to write a single word. I groan in frustration and rest my head in front of the keyboard. It has been so long since I wrote a cover letter. I managed to find my resume and polish that up a bit last night, but I am stumped when it comes to this.

How many ways can I say, "I'm a qualified candidate, please hire me!" And how can I sound less desperate?

Over the last month of job hunting, I have found a handful of Office Admin jobs and some Data and Business Analyst openings that are similar to my old position. Nothing really sounds promising yet, and I don't want to get stuck in the same rut I've been in for most of my adult life.

Burying myself in endless spreadsheets and building reports isn't fulfilling, at least not anymore. Without a deeper purpose, I fear I'll find myself growing jaded again.

Giving up, I close my laptop screen and drag myself to the kitchen. Spencer's mom had volunteered to take him to his PT appointment today so I could focus on the job hunt. I've sent off a handful of applications, but I am not feeling optimistic.

Standing before the sink, I look out across the yard. Summer is burning hot and dry, as evidenced by the browning grass and withered leaves of the oak trees. Man, do we need rain. Not having a job didn't bother me until recently. With Spencer regaining his strength, he's relying on me a little less. Now I'm left wondering what I'm supposed to do.

Blowing out a breath, I cross the kitchen and stare longingly into the fridge. I don't even know what I'm looking for. With everything going on, I have not gotten out of the house much, and the lack of food here is evident.

Spontaneously, I grab my phone and keys and decide to go for a drive. I shoot Spencer a quick text that I'm heading out to pick up groceries, just in case he beats me home.

At the store, I pick up the ingredients for chicken noodle soup and tomato bisque. Temperatures are forecasted to start cooling off this week, heralding the beginning of soup season. As I pass the baking aisle, I grab a few things to make a few loaves of homemade bread.

If I'm not working, I might as well be baking. Other than a few box cake mixes, I've never dallied with breads and pastries over the years. Might as well give it a shot. Who knows? Maybe I have a hidden talent and can open one of those cute farmhouse-style bakeries like in those corny movies they play at Christmas time.

I chuckle to myself as I add flour and sugar to my cart and wheel toward the checkout. The woman scanning my items is about my age with warm brown eyes and a kind smile.

"Did you find everything you were looking for today?" she says brightly.

"Mmhmm," I say with a slight smile and glance around awkwardly.

"It's a little brisk out today." She makes the obligatory comment about the weather.

Typical Midwestern that I am, I stifle the urge to make a comment about how it wouldn't be too bad if it weren't for the wind.

"Ah, but I'm no fan of the heat," I say instead, surprising myself with my friendly tone.

My wandering gaze lands on a flyer advertising kittens for adoption. Noticing my stare, the clerk nods toward the brightly colored paper.

"You a cat person?"

Gosh. I don't know if I ever thought about it. Spencer and I have never had a pet before.

"I don't know." I answer honestly, "What about you?"

"Oh, I have three myself: Miles, Max, and Madagascar."

I laugh at the unusual name, "Yeah, I've never had a cat before."

"Oh, they're great companions," she continues, ringing up my groceries, "I got Madagascar after my shoulder surgery. He was a big comfort during my rehab. He would just sit on my chest and purr for hours."

"My husband is recovering from a femur fracture," I say the thought out loud, as I grab my card from my wallet to pay.

"The shelter is just across the street if you're interested."

I thank her and leave the store with my bags. I deposit my purchases in the back seat and climb in behind the wheel, but my hand hesitates at the ignition.

I should take the groceries and head back home, but something is tugging at me. Maybe it was the fuzzy printed image on the flyer, but somehow, I find myself walking across the street.

The animal shelter is a grey steel-frame commercial building with large glass-paned windows in the front and a "Wipe Your

Paws" welcome mat at the door.

My hand hesitates on the doorknob for a moment before I step inside. I'm greeted by the sounds of happy yapping from the back and a cheerful receptionist at the front desk.

"Hi! Can I help you?"

"Um, I'm not sure. I saw your flyer in the grocery store. . ." I trail off awkwardly.

What am I doing here?

"Oh yes, the kittens that are ready for adoption. Right this way." She leads me through a door and into a narrow room lined with cages.

She points to an oversized crate where three rambunctious kittens pounce on each other, growling and gnawing on each other's ears. She begins rambling on about how the trio landed in their care and how much interest they have gotten.

I poke a finger through the bars, and it immediately gets swatted by a needle-sharp paw. The calico cuties are certainly adorable, but I think they're a bit too feisty. My attention begins to stray to the long rows of cages next to them.

I absently walk along, peeking into each one. Some are curled up, napping happily, and others come to greet me, sticking their noses through the grates and rubbing their faces along the cage doors. A few shy away, and one sleek black cat with yellow eyes hisses at me and cowers in the furthest corner of its enclosure.

"Ah, that's Dexter," the shelter worker murmurs beside me, "He's a sad case. He just came in from an abusive home. We're working to resocialize him."

I nod and continue to the furthest cage on the back wall, where a snow-white ragdoll sleeps inside a cat bed. The tag on his cage says "Samuel, Age 8." I may know very little about cats, but I do know that makes him a senior. Noting his date of arrival, I see he's been at the shelter for 3 years.

Samuel opens his sleepy eyes and stretches lazily. That's when I notice something odd about his oversized feet.

"Sam, there is polydactyl. So, he has extra toes on his front paws. He's been with us for a long time, such a sweetheart."

There's something old and quiet and comforting in his blue eyes that almost reminds me of my mother's ceramic cat.

"Would you like to hold him?"

I nod once without thinking.

The gal pops open the cage, and a second later, I'm holding this enormous mountain of fluff. The lazy thing lifts his face and nuzzles my cheek once before resting his head back in his paws.

That's it, I'm a goner.

Before I realize what's happening, I'm back at the front desk, signing paperwork and handing over the $25 adoption fee, when I hear the door swing open behind me.

"Taylor?" a familiar sweet voice calls.

My blood runs cold as I turn around and face the blazing eyes of my sister.

Chapter 19

"I'm glad I finally ran into you," Leslie says, "You haven't exactly been taking my calls."

I hang my head, "I'm sorry. I've just been dealing with a lot lately."

"Hey," she says, looking me squarely in the eye. "I'm not upset. But we need to talk, okay?"

I give her a sad smile and nod.

"I see you have your hands full at the moment," she says, glancing down to the small cardboard carrier in my arms, "But coffee tomorrow?"

"Sounds good."

She brushes past me and signs in at the receptionist's desk. I want to say more. Some kind of explanation for my distance, but the words catch in my throat. Tomorrow. I'll take this fur ball home, regroup, and face her in the morning.

A half hour later, I'm pulling into the driveway. It looks like Spencer is back from his physical therapy appointment. Boy, is he in for a surprise.

"Honey, I'm home." I call from the doorway, "I have a surprise for you!"

Spencer zips into the kitchen in his chair. Man, has he gotten adept at maneuvering that thing.

"What's up?" he says, looking curiously at the box I'm carrying.

Samuel takes this moment to let out a friendly meow. I pop open the lid, and he gracefully drops into Spencer's lap, purring like a diesel engine.

"Oh, hello," Spencer chuckles, "Who do we have here?"

"His name is Samuel."

Spencer cocks an eyebrow in my direction, the question on his mind written across his face.

"I was out on a grocery run and wound up adopting a cat." I lift my shoulders in an innocent shrug.

Samuel nuzzles his soft head into Spencer's neck, and I see my blue-collar, tough-as-nails welder melt like a pool of solder.

"Oh, you're friendly." He croons, stroking down the cat's back, "You're such a handsome kitty. Yes, you are."

"You're not mad?" I ask cautiously. "I mean, it's not at all like me to do something so impulsive."

Spencer flashes me the biggest grin. "Babe. I love him, and I'm happy to see you finding your spark back."

His words warm something deep in my soul. Yeah, I think everything is starting to look up.

* * *

I fiddle with the paper ring around my to-go cup. After running into Leslie yesterday, I thought long and hard about what I was going to say. But now that she's sitting across from me, every word has fallen out of my head.

"So, you volunteer at the shelter, huh?" I say stupidly.

"Yeah. Peter's firm is one of their biggest donors. I've taken my class on a few field trips there, too."

How did we become such strangers? I feel like I barely know her anymore.

I nod and try to come up with more small talk to ease the tension that seems to have sucked all the air out of the café.

"I'm sorry-"

"I'm sorry-"

We both blurt at the same time.

"What do you have to be sorry for?" I ask. "I'm the one who has been moody and distant and missed your shower."

"No, I have been so wrapped up in my own wedding, I couldn't see that you were struggling. I meant to come see you after Spencer's accident, but it's all been so awkward since the bachelorette party."

Emotions wrap tightly around my heart.

"Oh, Leslie, you should be happy about your wedding. I'm sorry I didn't let you in. I'm guessing Dad told you about my situation?"

She gives me a sad smile.

"He didn't give specifics. He just said you had been going through something for a while now."

I take a deep breath. Time to be brave.

"Spence and I have been trying to have a baby for a while. I miscarried a few months ago."

"Oh my God," her hand flies to her face, "The night of the party. I was teasing you about drinking."

I keep my eyes on my coffee, "I miscarried later that night, but I hadn't been given great odds of sustaining the pregnancy."

She reaches across the table and takes my hands in hers. A lone tear tracks down her flawless face.

"I wish you had told me. I'm so sorry you went through that on your own," she says with sympathy in her eyes.

"The worst part is just feeling like a failure," I confess, "Like my body can't do what it should be able to."

Leslie blows out a low breath, "Well, you're not alone. I understand how you feel."

I throw her a puzzled look. She gently squeezes my hands and looks down as if collecting her thoughts.

"It was early in our relationship. Peter and I had only been together for a few months. The thought of being a mom was utterly terrifying, and when I found out I was pregnant, I was convinced it would scare him off. But he vowed to stick it out and make things work."

She paused to collect her emotions.

"I almost felt relieved two weeks later when I started bleeding. Then, the guilt hit me. I could barely get out of bed for a month. I kept asking myself, how can I be so heartbroken over something I didn't think I even wanted? Peter stayed by my side through all of it. That's when I knew that he was the one."

"Here's to good men," I say, raising my coffee cup and tapping it against hers.

Cracking a smile, we both take a sip.

"I'm really sorry you went through that, Les." I say sincerely, "I wish you'd confided in me."

"I guess we both have that problem." She chuckles humorlessly, "And besides, you've spent enough time taking care of me throughout our lives. It was time to let someone else take the burden."

"Hey, look at me." I urge gently, "You have never been a burden. I'm sorry if I ever made you think that."

She smiles warmly, and the tension in her shoulders begins to relax.

"So, how is Samuel?"

Ah, yes, in less than 24 hours, the little white fluffball has already littered my house with shed hair, catnip, and toy mice that Spencer insisted we needed to pick up last night.

"He's doing great. Spencer completely adores him. I think they're going to be good for each other."

Leslie laughs, "It's hard to picture Spencer as a cat person."

I nod in agreement.

"I've missed this," I say suddenly. "We need to do this more often. We're sisters, after all."

My stepmother's words echo in the back of my mind: *You were never alone.*

I didn't know how right she was. All this time, I had so many people in my corner. If only I had looked. So much love, just out of reach.

Later that evening, I decide it's time to text Shelby. Maybe we, too, can repair what I broke.

Moments later, the brief and blunt reply comes.

I can't deal with this right now. I'm sorry.

I stare at the message on my phone screen as my feeling of peace dissipates, and an ill feeling takes root in my gut.

Despite my apology, Shelby is uninterested in reconnecting. Guilt has me in a chokehold as I recall the nasty things I said to her in the midst of my pain. I guess I can't say I blame her for keeping her distance. I feel the sting of her rejection, but I won't fall apart. For now, all I can do is give her space.

Chapter 20

I glance at my watch to see that it's nearing 5:00. Another month has passed, and still no job offer. At least I've found new ways to occupy my time. I chuckle as I turn back to the mountain of intake papers before me.

With Spencer now able to get around on crutches, he hasn't needed my assistance as much at home, which freed me up to volunteer at the animal shelter.

They were in desperate need of some administrative assistance, as most of their staff and volunteers primarily work to care for the animals. Recently, there has been an influx of stray cats and dogs in need of care, which has kept the regular shelter workers busy.

Julie, the receptionist who helped when I adopted Samuel, has been working around the clock to syringe-feed a litter of kittens who lost their mom after a recent thunderstorm. The little darlings don't even have their eyes open yet, and their chance of survival is slim, but Julie became instantly attached to the four orange tabbies.

I don't know if I've ever worked with a more dedicated and loving group of people. It has been a refreshing change from the competitive corporate world. Outside of Shelby, everyone in my old office was distant at best, but otherwise cold and conniving. While I don't miss the work, I do miss my best friend. Maybe more time and space will help. I worry about how she's coping with everything as she would now be in the third trimester of her pregnancy.

As I work through the stack of papers, digitizing each file and organizing them by date, I think about how simple life can be when you step out of the rat race. I sigh and glance up at the clock. It's almost time to head back to the house to make supper. I log out of the computer and make my routine rounds through the kennels and cages. I've gotten into the habit of saying goodbye to my new fur friends at the end of each shift. There's been something almost therapeutic about spending time with these animals. Without a home or a family to love them, we are all they have in the way of comfort. I've felt that way a lot in my life, so maybe I relate to them somehow.

Although I do wish I could give them each a better life, I know that isn't something I'm able to do. What I can do is make their time here a little better. That may mean sneaking Reginald the Great Dane an extra milk bone or giving a few extra pats to our resident Yorkie, Po.

Even though I'm better at numbers than paws, they have slowly wormed their way into my heart. It's crazy how I've gotten to know each of them in just a few short weeks, and crazier yet, that one fateful trip to the grocery store has changed my life so much.

Sighing, I pick my purse up off the desk and head to my car. As I drive, I think about how much my life has changed over the last few weeks. Leslie and I have continued to meet weekly over coffee, sometimes discussing wedding plans, other times talking about life itself. Somehow, without me realizing it, my baby sister became an adult.

I smile as I turn down the oak-lined street to our house. When I pull into the drive, I notice a light on in the garage. Curious, I kill the engine and investigate.

As I step through the walk-in door, I immediately hear a clanging sound followed by a few choice words.

"Spence?" I call.

"Damnit!" he hollers, whacking his head on the raised hood of his truck.

"Are you okay?" I ask, "What are you doing out here?"

"Well, the truck needs an oil change," he says, wiping his hands with a shop towel.

Grimacing, he leans heavily against the truck. I notice his crutches propped up against the toolbox just out of his reach.

"But we won't be needing the truck for a while." I say, "You won't be cleared to work for weeks."

The scowl on his face deepens, "I'm just so sick of being cooped up."

He pitches the towel into the engine bay, expressing his frustration. I raise my eyebrow in response.

"I just needed to do something, Baby. I'm going stir crazy."

"I can understand that. You never could sit still for more than a second." I chuckle, trying to make light of the situation, but I can see his mood is not lifting.

"Tell you what. You give me directions, and I'll change the oil."

He ponders for a second, then nods in agreement. I bring the crutches to his side, and he grips the handles and drags himself toward a nearby lawn chair. Exhausted by the movement, he drops into a seated position and immediately begins massaging his injured leg.

Readying myself, I strip off my knitted cardigan and set it on a pile of boxes near the door, then slick my hair back into a ponytail.

"Okay, what's first?"

"Alright, see that creeper down there? I need you to get down on it and slide under the truck. You're looking for the oil pan."

"On it," I say with far more confidence than I possess.

I lay back on the padded board he referenced and wheel myself under the chassis. Using my phone light, I shine it around the front of the truck until I locate the oil pan.

"Found it!"

"Okay, you're going to take this socket wrench," he says, kicking a tool toward me, "and loosen the drain plug."

I hmmm to myself as I fumble with the wrench.

"Once you get it loose, grab that metal pan beside you to catch the oil." Spencer directs.

Here goes nothing, I think, as I get to work on the oil plug. I get the wrench in place and tug once. It doesn't budge. I grit my teeth and pull even harder. Still no movement.

"I don't know if I can get it off," I say crossly.

Finally, the plug gives a little, and oil begins seeping around it. Then, a gush comes as the plug falls to the garage floor. I scramble for the metal pan, but still end up with oil splattered everywhere.

Hearing all the commotion, Spencer calls out, "Everything okay under there?"

"Just fine," I reply, watching the flowing black liquid.

Once everything has drained out, I wheel out from under the truck with the full pan of oil.

Spencer stifles a laugh at my grease-smeared cheeks and splattered clothes.

"Okay, boss. Now what?"

"Here, I've already prepped the new filter." He hands me a rounded orange canister. "You'll need this oil filter wrench to remove the old one."

The second wrench has an enormous mouth, large enough to grasp the filter. I nod and then roll back under the truck a second time.

Flashing my light again, I finally find the old filter along the side of the engine block. Gripping the wrench tightly, I settle it around the base of the filter and begin twisting.

"Ow!" I say as I scrape my knuckle in the process.

Expecting another brutal fight, I am surprised when the filter loosens easily.

"Ahh!" I squeal as oil lands near my mouth.

"Oh yeah, I forgot to tell you, a little might spill from the old filter."

"A little?" I snap sarcastically.

From across the garage, I hear his low laughter. I've missed that sound, even if the laughter comes at my own expense. At least I got him out of his sour mood.

Once I have the new filter in place, I tighten it down and replace the plug. Pulling myself from under the truck, I dust my hands off on my now-ruined pants.

"Whew." I sigh, "I think I deserve a beer now."

Spencer's eyes meet mine. "I don't think I've ever been more attracted to you than I am right now."

"Oh, stop it," I blush, batting my eyelashes in mock flirtation.

He pulls himself to his feet and grasps my filthy cheeks between his calloused hands.

"You're the most beautiful woman I've ever seen, and I'm so in love with you."

He brushes a featherlight kiss across my lips, and my knees wobble. It's been far too long since we have been this intimate. Too many roadblocks have kept us apart. First, grief, and then his accident. But it seems that he's on the road to recovery, and so is our marriage.

I dig my fingers into the front of his shirt and deepen the kiss. Oh, how this man makes me melt. His arms drop to my waist, and he tugs me flush against his body. Desire consumes me as I wrap my hands around his neck and moan softly into his mouth. I need him. I need to feel all of him.

Abruptly pulling his lips from mine, he gives me a wink.

"Now we add the oil."

* * *

When Leslie first told me after her New Year's Eve engagement that she was planning on an early October wedding, I thought she was crazy.

I myself had a short engagement, although I'm far less particular about such things. Leslie can be... well, a bit high maintenance.

But several months of hard planning and a lot of emotional baggage have led us here.

Gentle music projects from speakers in the high, vaulted ceiling. One hand nervously swishes the soft satin while the other clenches my bouquet of lilacs and baby breath. How I found myself in a second lavender bridesmaid dress, I'll never know.

The music continues as other bridesmaids and groomsmen enter the sanctuary ahead of us and filter from left to right.

Peter's brother Ryan looks just as uncomfortable as I do in a navy tuxedo with a light sheen of sweat across his brow. Swallowing my nerves, I loop my arm through his as the chapel doors open and 200 pairs of eyes swivel toward us.

They're not here to see me. I remind myself. I lift my gaze from the floor and begin the slow and steady march toward the altar. I concentrate on not walking too fast or trip on the hem of my dress.

I force myself to smile politely and nod to those we pass in the pews, awaiting the woman in white. The sound of Greensleeves buoys me to the end of the aisle. I've always loved the peaceful melody.

Love glistens in Spencer's eyes as I pass his seat. He throws me a wink that has heat creeping up my back and a blush pinkening my cheeks.

Reaching the steps, Ryan and I part ways — him to the right to stand beside Peter, and me to the left. I take my place next to Peter's sister Beth and two of Leslie's sorority sisters, whom I've come to know as Rory and Kelsi. The three of them were paired with some college friends of Peter's. Their names escape me.

The last to arrive: A pair of darling little girls in fluttery white tulle dresses. I smile as I remember Leslie fulfilling that role when Dad married Genie, and now it's her turn to marry the love of her life.

The music lowers as the pastor gestures for the congregation to rise as the first notes of Canon in D fill the chapel. My sister, draped in ivory lace, ascends the aisle on our father's arm. The cane is nowhere in sight, and yet he seems to walk with the grace of a much younger man. Something has breathed life into the feeble man he once was.

I remember standing in this very church so many years ago in a moment much different than this. Standing at that altar while Dad and Genie exchanged vows, I was filled with feelings of fear and dread. Among the crowd, I met Spencer's eyes and the promise radiating within their icy depths. I knew then he was the one I wanted to spend the rest of my life with. At least that has never changed.

My eyes wander to Genie sitting in the front row. Making the effort to get to know her these past few weeks has been a rewarding experience. I still regret the years I spent mired in my own heartache, not letting anyone in. She truly is a gem.

Two rows back, my faithful Spencer watches me. Always my rock. Gratitude bubbles up within me, not only for him but for this incredible family I've always had around me.

My sister and father embrace, and then he turns to take a seat next to Genie. Leslie takes Peter's hand as the ceremony begins. She looks so beautiful, a radiant replica of our mom. It almost takes my breath away.

Before exchanging vows, she turns to hand me her bouquet of snow-white roses, and a single tear rolls down my face. I try to swipe it away, careful not to smudge the perfect smoky eye Leslie helped me create this morning.

An eternity later, the pastor declares them husband and wife as Mr. and Mrs. Heller share their first kiss.

"Time of My Life" comes on the overhead sound system. My sister giggles as Peter lifts her off her feet, carrying her back down the aisle.

I chuckle, thinking back to our childhood movie nights each Saturday. Dirty Dancing was always a favorite. I believe my baby sister has found her Patrick Swayze and forever dance partner.

At the reception, I settle into my seat between Spencer and Dad at the family table. I sigh, relieved that I didn't embarrass my sister on her special day.

Spencer slings an arm around my shoulders, and I lean toward his touch. Despite some lingering pain, his mobility continues to improve, although he still relies on his crutches to some degree.

Country and pop love songs are piped into the event center, and my toes begin tapping to an old Wham number. Spence drops a soft kiss on my forehead before rising stiffly and shuffling to the men's room. Although I could be out hitting the bars with the rest of the wedding party, this is where my heart wanted to be. I wouldn't trade it.

I settle in to people-watch as guests mingle and grab snacks and drinks from the open bar.

"Oh, I almost forgot." My dad interrupts my thoughts.

He ducks down and pulls a small gift bag from underneath the linen tablecloth.

"Leslie wanted me to give you this."

Curious, I reach inside and pull a slim glass bottle out from the tissue paper.

My heart freezes. I recognize the stylized lettering on the label. It's Mom's perfume.

I flash back to the memory of us as kids, watching Mom dab some on before weekend dates with Dad. The scent would linger in the room long after they had departed. After she died, it was that bottle that held so much comfort. When I was troubled, I'd sneak into their room and find it in the box of her things, Dad left under the bed.

I remember one day catching Leslie playing salon with all of Mom's makeup and that bottle of perfume. Enraged that she was using something so sacred as a plaything, I laid into her. In the midst of the scolding, the bottle crashed to the floor and smashed on the hardwood.

We cleaned up the glass shards, but the room smelled like Mom for the next month. When the scent finally faded, it felt like I was losing her all over again.

I turn the bottle over in my hands, "Where…" my voice breaks.

"Apparently, she found it in a store on the East Coast when she and Peter visited his aunt a few weeks ago."

"I wonder how she even remembered," I muse, "That was so long ago."

Dad chuckles, "Oh, she remembers, apparently you were cross with her for weeks when she broke the original bottle."

I smile sadly. I was so caught in my own grief that I didn't even think about what 8-year-old Leslie was going through at the time. Fighting back tears, I spritz some on my wrist. Immediately, I'm wrapped in a familiar, comforting scent. My eyes close in silent gratitude.

***

My head is practically throbbing from incessant scrolling. It has been almost two months of job searching. I've been offered a few interviews, but none of them have panned out. This is getting exhausting. And frustrating.

I close my laptop screen and lose myself in thought. I had

a dream last night that I can't get out of my head. The details are hazy, overlapping in a fog. But I remember the theme: Forgiveness. I don't know why that keeps bugging me today.

I've done my best to seek forgiveness for everything I've put my friends and family through. Aside from Shelby, who has become a ghost, I feel I have made things right with everyone.

I think of Spencer, who is currently doing leg exercises in the living room with Samuel keeping a watchful eye from the nearby windowsill. Our relationship has been flourishing despite everything we've been through. It hasn't been easy, especially in those first few days after dropping his pain medication. But as he's progressed in his recovery, the pain has lessened, and he's regained his strength.

I never dreamed I'd have a relationship with my father as I do now. Spencer and I now make a weekly trip to Oak Hills for Sunday supper with Dad and Genie. Spencer's mom, Theresa, will occasionally join us as well. She has a touch more light in her eyes than those tedious days she spent looming over Spencer's hospital bed.

I think of Leslie, lounging on a honeymoon beach somewhere in the Caribbean with her new husband. Her sweet gift is one I will always cherish, and I told her as much when I helped her into the car before they sped off to the airport. Those prickly feelings of jealousy have vanished like the last traces of snow on a spring day.

As I continue down the list, I can't help but feel that there's something I'm missing. Perhaps there is another side to forgiveness — the ones whom I need to forgive.

Grabbing a scrap piece of paper and a nearby pen, I begin jotting down names. Those who have wronged me. Those who have caused hurt.

Dr. Hatfield: The one who made me feel two inches tall. The belittlement. The condescension. I feel like I wasted so many years on the wrong treatment. However, I came out the other side stronger than before.

Jenna: The Disney villain mistaken for a princess. I won't forget how she turned on Shelby and me. But in the end, it opened my eyes to the crap I had been dealing with for years without realizing how miserable it was making me.

Sandra: Sandra was the queen of workplace toxicity. No one taught me my worth that better than Sandra herself. Working for her all those years was barely tolerable, but I learned patience and, eventually, how to hold my own.

Benny Waldorf: The 8th grader who mercilessly teased me in junior high after I was smacked in the face with a volleyball during a scrimmage in gym class. Because of him, the name Taylor the Failure stuck with me for the next three years. His torment wounded a part of me that took years to heal, but that girl is gone now.

I read over my list and, one by one, try to let go of the pain each has caused. I slow my breathing and release the residual anger. This isn't quite as hard as I thought it would be. It feels like coming home from school with a backpack loaded with heavy textbooks and suddenly dropping it to the floor. Instant relief.

Finally, I jot one final name on the list: **Taylor Swanson.**

It's time to forgive myself. For everything. I know forgiveness is a choice, and I have to keep choosing it every day. But somehow this small step of letting go makes me feel so much lighter.

My phone rings, interrupting my inner peace. Answering, I hear an unknown voice on the line.

"Taylor, yes. This is Amanda Paulson with the Westland County Animal Shelter board of directors."

"Um, hi. How can I help you?"

"I know you've been helping a lot with our intake and adoption paperwork, and we think you'd be a great fit to run our community outreach and oversee our volunteer program. If you're interested, I'd like to offer you the position of Executive Director."

Momentarily mute, I process what's been said.

"Uh, yes, I'd be interested."

Amanda proceeds to fill me in on the job duties and salary details. I readily accept, and she leaves me with a note to come by in the morning for orientation, and we can get started. Giddy, I thank her for the opportunity and end the call.

Coming up behind me, Spencer throws his arms around me, still sweaty from his workout.

"How's the job hunt going, baby?" he asks lazily.

"I just got hired. I start tomorrow." I say, shellshocked.

* * *

Sitting cross-legged on the bedroom floor, I stretch out my middle finger, attempting to reach the correct fret on the neck of my mother's guitar. Dad dropped it off the other day during one of his regular visits. I had previously made a sarcastic remark about needing a new hobby now that my volunteer work at the shelter has resulted in a full-time position.

He said with a smile that there has always been music in me, as there was with my mother.

Now struggling to bend my fingers into the correct position, I am not so sure. I remember watching my mother's elegant hand dance along the guitar in a fluid motion, the other strumming in perfect rhythm, filling our home with beautiful Celtic music. She made it look effortless.

So far, I've dropped two picks into the body of the guitar by accident, and don't get me started on the sound coming from this thing. I've heard prettier music from Samuel at 2 a.m., when he accidentally gets locked out of the bedroom.

I hum along to a familiar old George Strait song as I attempt the chords.

I wince as I fumble the G note. This mournful song has taken on a special meaning. It may have been written about lost love, but somehow it has come to remind me of the child I lost. The bittersweet words comfort me, knowing she's in a safe place where the grass is green, and the sky is baby blue.

Samuel wanders into the room and begins grooming himself in the doorway, stopping when I begin to play again.

Despite the garbled chords, he seems to enjoy the soft melody, aggressively purring right along. Approaching, he begins nudging my strumming hand, begging for attention.

Laughing softly, I set aside the guitar for the day and scoop up the silky feline. I never thought I'd consider myself a cat lady, but there's some simple joy in stroking his soft fur, watching his dainty claws flex in and out as he enjoys a thorough scratching behind his ears.

I'm still amazed at how Samuel can transform from a regal senior cat in one moment into a frisky kitten in the blink of an eye. My new coworker, Julie, has told me that in all the years he was at the shelter, he never displayed such playfulness. It just goes to show you what a stable, loving environment can do for a lost soul. I'm evidence of that myself.

I glance at my watch. Spencer should be getting home any

minute. While light-duty work won't be starting for a few more weeks, his boss has asked him to take on a managerial role at the facility, which means a bit more desk work than he's used to.

Since he's been out of commission for so long, he jumped at the chance to do something productive. He has come so far with his physical therapy and has gained nearly all his mobility back. He still tires easily, but I'm in awe of what he's accomplished in a short amount of time.

He went from wheeling himself around in his chair to driving his truck and getting back into the gym again.

On the nearby nightstand, my phone rings, breaking through my thoughts. Rising to my feet, I drop Samuel on the bed with a final loving pat and reach for the phone.

It's Shelby.

I falter for a second, my heart racing with anticipation, before I slide my finger across the screen and lift it to my ear.

"Um. Hello?" My voice is uneasy.

I hear fast and heavy breathing on the other end and, finally, a strained voice.

"Taylor! I need you! Please hurry!"

Instant dread floods my body, and my veins ice over.

Chapter 21

My palms are slick with sweat as I clench the steering wheel, speeding toward the hospital.

"Taylor! Watch out!" My passenger bellows as I take a corner a touch too fast.

"Okay, don't you think that was a bit dramatic?" I say coolly.

"Try having a bowling ball squeeze its way out of you, then we can talk about dramatic!"

A yowl of pain cuts off her retort as another contraction slams into her.

"Breathe." I say gently, "We're almost there."

Her glare tells me she doesn't appreciate my coaching, but she's in too much pain to say anything.

The signs for the hospital appear up ahead, and I dart into the next lane to prepare for my turn. The jostling enrages Shelby even more.

"Seriously? Who taught you how to drive, Dale Earnhardt?"

I roll my eyes at the jab, but deep down, my stomach is tied in an overhand knot. Is she progressing too fast?

I must say I was shocked that I was the one she called when she went into labor. When I first arrived at her downtown apartment, the contractions were every 15 minutes, and now they're right on top of each other. She can make cracks about my speeding, but there's no way in hell I can handle her giving birth in my car. The blood alone would probably make me pass out.

"You just worry about keeping that baby in for a few more minutes," I joke, "I just got the upholstery cleaned."

She flashes a vulgar gesture, and I can't help but chuckle a bit as I guide the car into the first open spot I can find in the hospital parking lot. Fortunately, we won't have too much of a trek to the emergency room.

I throw open the door and dash to Shelby's side of the car. Huffing and puffing, she pulls herself up from the seat but immediately drops her hands to her knees in agony. I can actually see her belly tighten as the contraction rips a scream from her lungs.

"I can't do this," she sobs, panting in exhaustion.

"Wait here," I say with conviction.

I take off in a dead sprint toward the ER doors. Pushing down my crippling anxiety, I approach the front desk and ask a rather tired-looking receptionist for a wheelchair. Without batting an eye, she nods toward a courtesy chair in the lobby.

Racing back out the door with the provided chair, I help my miserable friend up off the pavement and begin wheeling her into the building.

Once inside, a flurry of activity begins. Questions fly at me that I have no idea how to answer. I have no clue how far along she is, the name of her doctor, or her birth plan. Shelby is not in any condition to speak more than a few grunted syllables.

Finally giving up, a nurse in pink scrubs begins wheeling Shelby to the maternity wing of the hospital.

The building becomes a maze as we rapidly pass room after room, turning corners, and finally arrive at an elevator.

In the delivery room, Shelby is directed to change into a hospital gown, which she does reluctantly with a little bit of assistance.

"Dr. Jensen is on call this evening, and she'll be with you in a few minutes," the nurse says as she checks Shelby's vitals and hooks up various sorts of monitors.

My heart stutters for a second. The last time I saw Dr. Jensen...

I squeeze my eyes shut. I don't want to think about that. I need to be here for Shelby, not drowning in the past.

"Holy Mother of Pearl!" Shelby screams as the nurse checks her for dilation.

"Seems like you're at about a 6, so it's going to be a while, yet." The nurse says matter-of-factly.

"What do you mean, 'it's going to be a while,'" Shelby barks. "When can I get an epidural?!"

"We have to do an hour of IV fluids before we can place the epidural. I can get that started if you want."

"I want!"

I watch this exchange, not entirely sure if I should step in. And frankly, I'm a little frightened by my friend's sudden personality shift.

The nurse hurries off to retrieve the necessary items. I'm sure they've been here a thousand times, but it's easy to imagine the nurse fleeing from Shelby's rising temper.

I cautiously approach the bed, where a sweating, puffing Shelby is gritting her teeth against another wave of pain.

"I'm so scared," she confesses through her grimace. "I don't think I can do this. I called my mom and sister, but they won't make it here from Texas until tomorrow."

"You were right to call me," I say, lowering myself down to the edge of her bed. I take her right hand in mine, and she latches on with a tight squeeze. Finally, as the contraction releases, she flops back against the mattress in exhaustion.

"He didn't want anything to do with me," she whispers miserably up at the ceiling.

"Who didn't?" I ask.

"Her father." She says, resting her hand on her swollen belly, "He wants nothing to do with this baby."

My heart fractures. To be rejected in such a way and to face motherhood on her own.

"Oh, Shelb," I say, giving her hand a slight squeeze.

"I texted him the day after I told you. First, he accused me of lying and trying to trap him. After I convinced him that I was telling the truth and that I wanted to give him the option of being involved, he just said it wasn't his problem and bailed."

The crack in my heart widens with guilt over my callous words.

"I said such awful things to you. I'm so sorry, Shelby. I had no idea what you were going through."

"We both were going through some awful things."

"It doesn't excuse what I did."

Shelby tenses again, and I brace for her vice-like grip on my hand.

"Let's just focus on getting this baby out of me." She smiles through the pain.

"I got you," I say, placing my free hand on her shoulder as she leans into me.

The nurse materializes again and begins prepping Shelby's arm for the IV. My stomach roils, but I try to tamp down my nausea as the needle punctures her tattooed wrist and the nurse tapes on the IV port.

Shelby's face drains of color during the procedure, but she doesn't otherwise react.

As the minutes tick by, I help her make slow laps around the room, scooting along her IV pole and providing frequent sips from her hospital mug. She bounces on an oversized yoga ball for a while until her hips ache. We pass the time making small talk between bouts of pain. She cracks jokes about her newfound self-employment and the state of her love life.

"I did meet a nice man recently. He's an investment banker, so a step above the usual scum I go for. We'll see if he's still interested in me now." She says, gesturing to her belly with a slight smile.

One hour and a shift change later, a new nurse is giving her another cervical check before they send for the anesthesiologist.

Shelby winces but doesn't cry out this time. But as the nurse announces she's only at a 7, a fire lights in her eyes.

"All this time, and I'm only at a 7?"

"Babies come in their own time," the nurse says gently.

I try my hardest not to snicker at Shelby's exaggerated eye roll, and I imagine she's biting down a nasty retort.

After another 15 minutes of bouncing, laps, and deep breathing, the anesthesiologist and another new nurse arrive to begin placing the epidural. They instruct Shelby to sit on the edge of the bed and lean forward. I support her arms and shoulders and try to avert my eyes from whatever they're inserting in her back.

"You must remain still, even if you have a contraction," the nurse orders tightly.

"How the hell am I supposed to hold still during a contraction?" Shelby grumbles.

From the corner of my eye, I can see the needle go in, and I gulp audibly and drop my gaze to the floor.

"Yow!" Shelby shrieks as her leg jolts.

"You have to hold still," the nurse reminds.

"I didn't do that," Shelby says.

"Ah, got a zinger, did ya?" The anesthesiologist chuckles a bit, "That can happen. Just hold tight as best you can."

The needle probes again as Shelby's leg twitches a second time.

"Are you about done poking around back there?" she snarls.

"Almost finished."

The grim-faced nurse assisting him looks less than patient but remains silent as they finish up the placement.

Once everything is taped down and the fluid starts running, color returns to Shelby's face as the pain slowly washes away.

"How are we feeling now?" the nurse asks, checking her vitals.

"Much better," Shelby breathes deeply, "I have to apologize, I'm not usually this snappy."

The nurse casts her knowing smile, "I've seen a thing or two," she says before breezing out of the room.

The hours tick by as Shelby rests comfortably in bed. I doze in and out of sleep on the nearby couch, interrupted periodically by the nurses who come to check her progress. By 1:00 a.m., she was at 8 centimeters, and by 2 a.m., she reached a 9. Shelby's war cries had now been reduced to soft grunts at each contraction.

At 2:30, her voice wakes me, "Aw, man! I wet the bed!"

I toss aside the thin hospital blanket and hurry to her side.

"Girl, you have a catheter in. I think your water broke," I say, pressing the call light.

A nurse quickly appears and confirms my suspicion, indicating the time is nearing. Everything starts happening at double speed. Dr Jensen is called, nurses shuffle in and out, setting everything up. Within minutes, Shelby's feet are in stirrups with a nurse on either side of her and chipper Dr. Jensen is poised between them.

"Shelby, are you ready to have a baby?" Dr. Jensen says.

She nods nervously and bears down. I grip her hand tightly, wipe sweat from her brow, and offer her spoonfuls of crushed ice between each push.

I somehow can't wrap my mind around the miracle happening before my eyes. With each contraction, I meet her eyes, breathe deeply with her, and brace myself against her forceful grip. Then it is rinse, lather, repeat. At 3:07 a.m. on October 20th, a baby's cry pierces the sterile hospital air.

My throat chokes up, and I swipe at my eyes as they place a squalling, red-faced newborn on Shelby's chest.

"She's perfect," Shelby sobs, dropping soft kisses on her daughter's forehead.

The infant, lulled by the familiar melody of mom's heartbeat, calms to soft cooing.

"What's her name?" a nurse asks, holding a blank hospital wrist band.

"I haven't decided," Shelby says, overcome with emotion. "Isn't that terrible? What mother doesn't know what to name her child?"

"What about Faith?" The words are out of my mouth before

I realize what I'm saying.

Shelby's eyes snap to mine.

"Isn't that the name you picked out for your daughter? Your mother's name?" she asks carefully.

Bless her, I swear she remembers everything I've ever told her.

I nod slowly, "It's okay, I don't think I need it. And besides, Faith Marie Peters" has a nice ring to it.

Shelby smiles and caresses the tiny girl's cheek, "Then Faith Marie, she shall be."

Moments later, the name is secured around the baby's perfect tiny ankle.

* * *

The thought of having friends and family gathering in my house would have historically scared the living shit out of me. But here I am hosting a Thanksgiving dinner, complete with a roasted turkey and all the fixings.

Spencer has graciously stepped in to carve the turkey while I spend some time with my new niece. Faith's dark blue eyes are wide and searching despite being sound asleep only moments ago. I brush my knuckle down her soft, rounded cheek and ruffle her downy head.

Her lips curve upward in a tiny smile. I'm told it's probably from gas, but I'll tell myself that she enjoys my presence. My heart still aches like a fading bruise, but the pain mingles with a feeling of utter joy.

A few others have recently arrived, but she has had all of my attention. I can't even fathom that at one time I was so incredibly jealous of Shelby. I can't imagine harboring ill will after holding this angel in my arms.

"Okay, Auntie. Hand her over. Baby's gotta feed." Shelby says, nodding toward the infant who has started suckling on her thumb.

Gently lifting Faith to her mom, I rise from my seat and begin to mingle with the others who have gathered in my living room.

"Hey, sis!" Leslie says, offering a hug.

Post-honeymoon, Leslie and Peter have recovered from their tropical sunburns and have settled nicely into married life. My sister and I have continued our weekly coffee shop ritual, and it's surprising how much we didn't know about each other.

For example, I had no idea she went skydiving once in college and wound up throwing up midair. Swapping embarrassing stories and chatting about our personal failures has helped bridge the gap that had grown between us. I'm not sure we've ever been this close, and I see her in a different light now. No longer the baby sister I have to protect, she's now a full-fledged woman worthy of my respect.

"How's the old married man?" Spencer teases, pumping Peter's hand.

I roll my eyes, knowing full well that Spencer despised those same comments when we were first married. Peter doesn't seem to mind as they launch into a lengthy conversation about college football.

Leslie turns from their conversation and meets my eye.

"How are you doing with things?" she murmurs, motioning toward Shelby, feeding a very hungry Faith.

After the two of them were released from the hospital, I've been dropping by a few times a week to help Shelby out. While being a sweet and peaceful babe during the day, Faith is a bit of a night terror, which has left Shelby stressed and depleted. I've brought food, helped with household chores, and taken the baby to allow her some rest time. It has been rewarding in an unexpected way.

For so long, I thought the only way to reach this level of fulfillment was to have my own children, but I have discovered that there are other ways to find joy. And that maybe my journey isn't over. Last week, I called Dr. Jensen and got a referral to the fertility clinic. I haven't found it in myself to make that appointment, but it's nice to know I have options. I still may never get to experience motherhood for myself, but I know that I have so much love in my life right now.

"Yeah," I say in response to Leslie's question, "I'm doing great, actually."

"It was incredibly sweet to offer up your baby name," She smiles softly, "Mom would have been honored."

She gives my shoulder a gentle squeeze before slipping off to refill her wine glass.

I walk toward the kitchen counter, where an assortment of cookies, appetizers, and dips are laid out buffet-style. Genie is perusing the spread, adding dabs of this and that to her paper plate.

"Thanks for coming," I tell her.

"Oh, darlin', thanks for the invite. It does your father good to be around you girls," she smiles wistfully at my dad, who has gotten swept up in the football conversation.

Somehow, the very tired, frail man who bravely stepped into Spencer's hospital room a few months ago has been replaced by a much younger, vibrant man. I watch him talk animatedly with his hands, no cane in sight, and it makes my heart sing.

As everyone finds their place at the table, I think this is

as close as it gets to a Hallmark holiday. Feeling a surge of courage, I step to the front of the room and begin rapping my plastic fork against the side of my wine glass.

Anxiety grips me as every eye in the room swivels to me.

"Uh, Th-thank you for being here." I feel a heat creeping up my neck.

I take a fortifying breath before continuing. "Social gatherings are not my forte, and neither is public speaking, so please bear with me. As all of you are aware, it has been a difficult year for our family. We were faced with a couple of trying situations. I, personally, didn't handle those situations the best at times, and I apologize for that. But all of you have been there for me. For us. Spencer and I are incredibly grateful to have you all in our lives."

I pause as my voice quavers.

"Now, without further ado. Let's eat that bird!"

I raise my glass and take a sip as those in the room cheer and clap. From the far side of the room, a small voice begins humming: Shelby to her squalling daughter.

Next to her, Genie begins singing in a low voice, *"You are my sunshine, my only sunshine."*

Before long, the entire table has joined in the sweet lullaby. As the final note fades, Faith closes her eyes and drifts to sleep.

Chapter 22

Winter in the Midwest can be brutal, and the closer we get to Christmas, the more I have been fighting the blues.

Genie brought me a small box tied with ribbon yesterday. Inside was a beautiful white glass ornament with angel wings. The inscription reads, "The smallest lives leave the biggest holes in our hearts."

A tear slipped down my cheek as I placed it on the tree – evidence that the grief never fully leaves us, even as we hope for better days ahead.

While I have a Christmas tree with lots of pretty packages and children's toys beneath it, that singular ornament is a reminder that those plush teddy bears aren't for a child in my home. I should be holding an infant today, but she slipped away before she could spend Christmas with me.

I adore being Faith's auntie, but I still long for my own baby. For weeks now, I've stared at the business card on my fridge: Heartland Fertility Specialists. I don't know why I keep hesitating. I've picked up my phone at least 5 times over the last month, meaning to dial, but something stops me every time.

Spencer hasn't pressed me. He thinks he put too much pressure on me last time, even though most of that urgency was created by my own anxiety. Now that he's fully recovered, we've been trying again. But we both know our chances are slim. For now, that's okay with me. I'm not sure my heart can withstand another loss so soon after everything we went through.

I glance down at my cluttered desk. I've been in this role for barely two months, and it has been nonstop. Now that we're in the height of the holiday giving season, we have had an influx of donations and volunteers. Both are great things, but that means more paperwork and longer days.

And then there is our big fundraiser next week. I pitched the idea of a 'Bark'mas Fashion Show, where design students from the local college could model their outfits on the catwalk, along with the dog or cat of their choosing. It would be a great partnership that gives the kids an opportunity to showcase their work and gain exposure while also hopefully boosting adoptions for us.

We've invited fashion experts from across the state to serve as a panel of judges, and the winner gets a $5,000 scholarship to continue their degree. The outfits will be auctioned off, and the students will split the proceeds with the shelter. We are also running discounted adoption fees for any animal that participates in the show. This all might be a total flop, and I'll be laughed out of the building. But so far, the community seems really excited by it.

At that moment, Julie burst into my office. She's back to covering the front desk at the moment, but has also blossomed into my unofficial marketing assistant.

"Taylor!" Her eyes dance with excitement. "The tickets are sold out! We're going to have a full auditorium for 'Bark'mas!"

"That's awesome!" I stand up from my desk.

There's so much to do and only a week left to do it. I brief Julie on the last-minute details so we can get the programs printed.

"I'm also going to call the caterer with an updated headcount and double-check when the venue opens for setup."

Julie nods, checking items off her meticulously organized list.

"Okay, while I'm out on lunch, I'm going to swing by the floral shop to pick up the thank-you baskets for the judges. Oh, and I'm going to call Gary this afternoon to secure transportation of the animals to the event and back."

"Good thinking!" I say, smiling brightly, "We totally got this."

Not sure if I'm trying to psyche myself up or her. Would a high-five be cheesy and uncalled for right now? Probably. Don't be weird, Taylor.

Julie just grins and bustles out the door, determined to tackle her To Do list.

I drop back into my office chair and pause for a moment in quiet satisfaction. I pick up my phone and select one of my favorites.

"Hey you!"

"How's that beautiful niece of mine?"

Shelby's laugh sounds like the tinkling of a Christmas bell. "Perfect, as usual."

"Well, of course she is." I laugh right back, "How's the tummy time going?"

"Ugh. She hates it. But today, when I picked her up, she

smiled at me for the first time. Like, really smiled. So maybe she'll forgive me for making her do it."

I chuckle warmly, "How's your newest client?"

Ever since being let go from Apex, Shelby has been doing freelance work for some businesses in town. I'm glad her marketing genius is finally being recognized by others.

"You mean the client who doesn't even have a website because in his mind it's still 1995?"

"Yikes."

"Yeah. He thinks a few printed flyers and an ad in the newspaper are all he needs. I got my work cut out for me on this one."

"You'll get him to come around. You have a persuasion about you."

Shelby snorts, and I can almost hear the eye roll through the phone. "I'm serious, I learned everything I know from you. I wouldn't be sitting here now without you."

"Thanks, Tay. I just feel like I'm wasting my life right now. What am I doing designing ads for Mom and Pop shops?"

I pause, thinking through her situation. "Maybe you can start doing some consulting work? You have years of experience that others can tap into. You can do more than just design work. The strategy side is truly your superpower."

"Yeah. Maybe you're right. I never thought of it that way."

We wrap up our phone call with a promise to do lunch next week. Then I get back to the quickly growing number of unread emails before me.

* * *

I giggle as a troupe of Kindergarten elves cross the stage and begin their comical rendition of "Grandma Got Run Over by a Reindeer."

I did not expect to have this much fun at an elementary school Christmas pageant. I was a bit skeptical when Leslie invited me to watch her second-grade class perform, but these kiddos are so adorable.

My chest begins to tighten, but the pain eases as the children begin a lively dance routine that is wildly out of sync.

By the time the children exit the stage, my sides ache from laughter. The evening passes, and I feel my Christmas spirit rising with each performance.

A fourth-grade class takes its place on the stage and softly harmonizes the opening lines of "Silent Night."

A wave of nostalgia washes over me as the stage lights dim. Every year, Mom would pull Leslie and me into her rocking chair and read us "The Night Before Christmas." Once Leslie started to get drowsy, she'd lower her voice and hum the familiar Christmas carol until her little eyes closed.

Dad would come and carry my baby sister off to her room, and I'd beg to stay up late in hopes of catching a glimpse of Santa Claus. Soon, I too would be drifting off to sleep, lulled by the melody.

As the tiny choir on stage sings out *"holy infant so tender and mild,"* I catch Leslie's eye through the crowd. Her eyes shine with a dampness that I'm sure mine mirror.

After the show, we embrace for a long time in silent melancholy. But Christmas is about joy, so we put our sorrow aside and laugh and joke about the funniest moments of the night.

My heart still feels leaden as I drive home. I can't exactly put my finger on the root cause. But something draws me to my bookshelf and the well-worn journal. I've read through most of it now. The years of grief following my brother's death and my parents' trying desperately to start over. I ached with empathy for what she must have endured.

I flip to where I last left off — one of the final entries.

December 24, 2000

Taylor brought home a particularly nasty stomach bug from school last week. I've been feeling terrible all week and finally broke down and went to the clinic. I wound up in the office of a very rude Dr. Hatfield, who is new and has zero bedside manners.

He walked in and abruptly announced that I'm not sick, I'm pregnant! I couldn't believe it. After losing Caleb and all these years of trying, I have given up on having any more children. I've grown content in this life with Bradley and Taylor. We have a wonderful life, just the three of us.

I'm overjoyed, of course, but I can't help but feel apprehensive. What if I lose this one too? What if Taylor doesn't adjust well to having a sibling? What if I can't handle being a mother to two children?

I haven't told Brad yet. A part of me still doesn't quite believe it. I think I will tomorrow. What a special Christmas gift.

Oh, Mom. All this time, I had no idea that we shared the same fears, the same wounds. I miss her so much right now, but I'm suddenly comforted in knowing that I'm going to be okay.

* * *

Nervous energy flutters in my belly as I watch a model in a fluorescent orange jumpsuit strut down the runway with a Sphinx cat perched in her arms.

The concept is so absurd that it actually works. I know less than nothing about fashion, and being in the Midwest, we aren't exactly at the forefront of the industry. Yet, somehow, this seems to be working. The audience is engaged, cameras are flashing, and the occasional "aww" erupts when a particularly cute animal walks out.

Henry, the 12-week-old labradoodle puppy, has been the crowd's favorite. I wouldn't be surprised if we are swimming in adoption applications for him, come Monday morning. I smile to myself as the final stylist shows off her buccaneer-inspired design with our resident macaw perched on her shoulder.

The audience chuckles as they exit the stage, and applause rises through the auditorium. I did it. I can't believe I pulled off this crazy stunt. As folks linger about after the show, top off their drinks, and sign donation pledge cards, I bask in the glow of success.

From the corner of my eye, I spot Spencer moving toward me through the throng of suits and cocktail dresses.

"For the director," he jokes, producing a large bouquet of red roses.

I blush. "Oh, hardly. It was all Julie."

I gesture to my right, where my fearless assistant beams. The light from the nearby Christmas tree sparkles in her gray eyes.

Julie chuckles, "The true stars of tonight's show were Henry and Sasha."

Indeed, Sasha Evans's powder blue fairy dress received the highest score from the judges, and paired with the sweet puppy, the duo stole the hearts of everyone in attendance. The scholarship was well deserved.

Julie and I chat briefly to ensure the final details of the night go off without a hitch. As the after-party starts to wane, Spence and I slip away from the noise.

On the walk back to the car, he captures my hand in his, our fingers entwining like they did when we were kids.

"I'm so impressed by you," he whispers into the quiet evening air.

"You know what?" I say, stopping for a moment. "I am, too."

* * *

A toddler zips past me at lightning speed. There are exactly 3 of them running around, and I'm losing track of which one is which. Needing some air, I slip out the screen door and take a seat on the patio. The weather is mild for late December, but the chill in the air does my mind some good.

It has been a few years since I've attended a family Christmas, and apparently, my cousins have been prolifically reproducing. I faintly remember my cousin Brook being pregnant the last time I saw her, and now she has a daughter in preschool and a newborn son, meanwhile her younger sister Becky has 2-year-old twin boys.

I remember spending more time with Brooke and Becky when we were little. We were all within a few years of each other, and at the time, we lived 3 blocks away. Shortly before Mom's cancer diagnosis, Dad's brother Ben and his wife Karen moved their family to Colorado. I was about 10 at the time, and I thought my life was over. I always wondered if there had been some big falling out, because I didn't see my cousins again until Mom's funeral. We used to write letters back and forth and friended each other on Myspace, but over the years, we drifted apart.

It's only been the past 5 years or so that Ben and Dad

have reconnected, and they've all started coming back for Christmas. Of course, I've been absent for 3 of those years. Until now.

It would be easy to envy my cousins for the lives they have now. They're starting families with adorable babies and are married to successful men, an engineer and a software developer. But over the course of the evening, I've gotten to visit with them, and they've both had their struggles through motherhood. Some hilarious and some heartbreaking.

"There you are," Dad says, sidling up beside me.

I smile, lifting my wine glass to my lips.

"It was getting a bit hectic in there." I motion toward the house.

"Yes, indeed," he chuckles softly. "Ah, but it's music to these old ears. This house is too quiet most days."

Nodding, I glance up at the scattered stars and the Milky Way painted across the night sky.

"I wanted you to have this," he says, handing me a wrapped box.

"Oh, Dad. You didn't need to get me anything."

Setting my glass aside, I peel back the paper to reveal a small leather-bound journal, almost identical to the one I received four Christmases ago.

"Mom kept another journal?" I breathe. But when I thumb through the pages, I find them to be pristine. Untouched.

"I found this the other day when cleaning the garage. The first two pages were stuck together."

He opens the cover, revealing a single journal entry dated *December 24, 2006.* Two weeks before Mom died.

"I believe it was the last thing she ever wrote. Shortly after that, her hands were too weak to hold a pen."

Silent tears slip down my cheeks as I read her words – her final wishes for me.

Dad presses a kiss to my forehead. "I thought … maybe you could write your next chapter in the journal she never finished."

I let out a shaky breath, "I'm not sure anyone will ever want to read it," I say with a humorless chuckle.

He smiles, his face lined with warmth. "Then write it for yourself."

"Thanks," I say, surprising myself when I pull him in for a hug.

Dad turns to head back inside when he stops and glances over his shoulder at me.

"One more thing, kid." He lowers his voice. "I want you to know that it's okay if you try again for a baby. It's also okay if you don't. If you and Spencer adopt a baby or have one of your own, we'll love them either way. I think you'll be a wonderful mother, no matter what path you choose."

My eyes sting, and my throat closes as I nod. "I know that, Dad."

He shuffles back into the house, and I take a few moments to compose myself before heading inside as well.

The evening carries on with the boisterous unwrapping of gifts and lively chatter. While social situations typically wear me out, tonight's gathering has left me with an unexpected lightness.

I can't exactly put my finger on what has changed, but there is something different in the air.

As we exchange goodbyes, hugs, and a few recipes as everyone shuffles toward the door, my heart feels full. The drive home feels peaceful after the noise and chaos of the day.

When we arrive home, we unload the car and place the many boxes of leftovers in the fridge.

We each steal one last bite of cherry cobbler, and Spence, never forgetting his faithful friend, tosses Samuel a treat.

"You heading to bed now, baby?" Spencer asks from his spot on the floor, rubbing Samuel's tummy.

"You know? I might take a quick shower. My stomach is kind of turning all of a sudden." I say with a small knot forming in my gut.

"Too much wine," Spencer says with a wink.

"Probably more like too much sugar and cheese." I say with a groan, "Getting old is the worst."

Spencer chuckles as he approaches and plants a kiss on my forehead.

"As long as I get to grow old with you, I'll be happy with that."

I pull Spencer in for an extra second just to relish that closeness one minute more. Then I pull away and head to the bathroom.

I can hear Spencer continue teasing Samuel with a feather duster in the other room as I turn on the faucet. Pulling open the bottom drawer to look for a new bottle of conditioner, I spot an unopened pregnancy test.

The pink packaging stares me down. A reminder of where I've been and what I've been through. I stare right back, challenging it. Impulse hits me as I tear open the wrapper.

Exactly three minutes pass before tears begin falling down my face like rain on a windshield.

"Spencer!" I scream.

Footsteps thunder toward me as the door swings open.

"Baby? What's wrong?"

I have no words. Instead, I extend my hand and reveal two bright pink lines.

He takes the test with trembling hands and stares in utter disbelief before collapsing in my arms.

A miracle.

Epilogue

One Year Later

Endometriosis.

The diagnosis splits my chest like an axe as tears well up behind my eyes. I felt something wasn't right, but hearing the words hurts more than I expected.

"The likelihood of conceiving naturally will be next to impossible."

I can't fully comprehend the words.

"Impossible?" I ask helplessly.

"At this point, the best options are surrogacy or adoption."

My throat closes, and my words dry up.

"I mean, if surrogacy is an option, I.."

"I could never ask you for that," Leslie interrupts, "And besides, Peter and I have already discussed this. I'm weirdly excited to begin the adoption process."

I try to read her face to catch her in a lie, but warmth is

shining in her eyes.

"Am I disappointed that I won't have kids of my own? Yes. Does it suck to get such a crappy diagnosis? Yes. But at least now I know what's going on."

I nod in understanding, pulling my peacoat tighter against the frigid air. The years I spent searching for reasons behind my infertility were hell. There is some sort of peace that comes with knowing *what* you're facing, even if you don't know how to battle it.

I lift my coffee cup for the last sip before tossing it in a nearby trash can. A gust of arctic wind hits us as we make our way down the sidewalk and toward the parking lot.

Our weekly coffee date has been put on a nearly 6-month hiatus, and today's outing is perhaps a first step in reviving it. Life has been hectic. For both of us.

The newlywed phase has started to fade, but between school and her periodic bouts of pain, she has had a lot on her plate. I lift up a silent prayer that the doctors can find her some relief.

"Hey, how are the plans coming for the new center?" Leslie turns to me abruptly, changing the subject.

"Great," I say, clapping my gloved hands together for warmth, "We've secured about 80% of the funding, and we're set to break ground next April."

"That's got to be exciting!"

That's the truth. Our current shelter building has had a plethora of issues over the past year. An early spring storm damaged the roof, and the subsequent water leak damaged some drywall. Then over the summer, our AC unit went out, leaving it sweltering hot in the steel frame building. Animals had to be shuttled to other centers and foster homes until we got the unit back up and running.

It has been a long year of applying for grants, schmoozing potential donors, and running fundraising campaigns, but we're about to take it across the finish line. Never in the world would I have pictured myself in this position, but I have found such satisfaction and purpose in this work.

Although some of the more social parts of the job can still be draining to my soul, all I have to do to recharge is take my nightly stroll through the animals in my care. Having that in mind is more than enough reason to keep going.

Reaching our parked SUVs at last, we hug and exchange goodbyes, and "we should do this again."

I wave as we exit the park. Leslie turns left toward her midtown condo while I make a right toward the nearest shopping center. I have a few things to pick up for our upcoming holiday party and some last-minute Christmas shopping.

Spencer is seriously the hardest person to buy for. He is a big fan of the practical gift, but he just goes and purchases whatever he needs. My gifts typically wind up being overly sentimental, personalized things that wind up collecting cobwebs on the shelf, or boring items like socks and new work gloves that are not very exciting to gift.

After last Christmas, we made a pact to simply do away with gift-giving, as we both are terrible at it. But that was before everything changed.

After what feels like hours of perusing shelves, I finally head to the front of the store and ring up my items at the self-checkout.

"Taylor, I thought that was you." A familiar voice rings out behind me in line.

Glancing up, I almost don't recognize my former colleague,

Jenna, without her signature blonde bob and low-cut blouse.

"Jenna, how have you been? You look good."

I mean it, too. Her now shoulder-length hair has faded to her natural brown, and her makeup is lighter than her normal dark-rimmed eyes and red lip. Despite her tamed-down appearance, she can still make a knitted sweater and blue jeans look sophisticated.

"You too," she says somewhat awkwardly.

With a growing sense of unease, I finish scanning my last items and swipe my card to pay.

I turn to acknowledge her as I leave, but before I can get out any parting pleasantries, she grips my arm.

"Taylor, I just want you to know I'm sorry for what I did. I got swept up in the competition, and I turned my back on what really matters."

Stunned, I don't say anything for a moment.

"We all were friends once. I miss that. The office sucks without you guys."

I meet her eyes and, I think, truly see her for the first time. Just a woman who was thrown into a dog-eat-dog world and taught to fight and cheat her way out. I think now I just see someone who is tired of playing the game.

"Then maybe it's time you get yourself out of there."

Her eyes drop to the floor, "I've actually been thinking about that. The one bright spot is that Sandra got fired last week."

"Oh?" I say, fighting back a smug smile.

"Yeah, corporate found out she was altering her marketing reports." Jenna rolls her eyes.

"Honestly, leaving there was the best thing that could've happened to me." I say in earnest, "There's life outside those four walls. You just have to be brave enough to step off the hamster wheel."

Sadness lingers in her eyes as she takes in my words.

"It was good to run into you," I say genuinely, and gather my bags to leave.

"Oh," I turn back around, "I forgive you, Jenna."

While her apology can't erase everything that happened, I've decided to leave the past where it belongs.

* * *

"Wait. She actually said that?"

"Yes," I confirm for the fourth time.

"Was she at least wearing like ratty pajama pants and an old gym shirt?"

I fight the urge to roll my eyes, "No, Shelby."

"Or missing a front tooth or something?"

I heave a deep sigh, "No, she was perfectly put together."

"Damn. Did she at least cry? Or grovel?"

I wearily scrub my hand over my face. "No, she just gave a genuine apology, and I forgave her."

"You what?! You forgave that viper?"

"What good would it do to hold a grudge? I'm a grown-up. She's a grown-up. I used to think *you* were a grown-up..."

I hear her snort on the other end of the phone.

"Fine." She gives in. "I'm just not ready to forgive her yet. Does that make me petty?"

"I love you, Shelb. But yes, you're being petty."

"Oo, I gotta go. He just texted."

I smile. "You need to bring the elusive Mr. Investment Banker to our party next week!"

"Yeah, yeah," Shelby says, brushing off my nagging.

For months, I've heard about her new love interest, but she's been hesitant to make an introduction. She promises she's finally ready for him to meet Faith, but she's been understandably protective of my toddling little niece.

"Give Faith some kisses for me. Love you!" I say quickly before the line goes dead.

***

After a quick shower, I dress silently in our en-suite bathroom. Slipping on my watch, I catch a glimpse of myself in the still-fogged-up mirror. I smile softly and switch off the flat iron, opting to let my hair dry into its natural waves instead.

I used to loathe this dishwater blonde hair and these boring grey eyes, but somehow, I've come to accept and appreciate them.

I spritz myself with Mom's perfume, slip on a pair of simple crystal stud earrings, and dab a touch of concealer under my eyes. After a few swipes of eyeshadow and mascara, I'm good to go.

I give myself one last perusal in the mirror as I hear a low voice drawing nearer.

Spencer steps into the bathroom, animatedly talking to someone and then quickly ending the call.

"Spence, you're still not ready to go? People will be arriving any minute," I chastise.

"Baby!" he says with glittering eyes, "Dan has agreed to a full partnership! With his help, Peter's investment, and your brilliant marketing mind, our welding shop will be off the ground in no time."

My heart lifts. He has been working on convincing his

longtime friend and coworker to go into business together for weeks. I'm so happy for him to finally see his dream realized.

"That's amazing, babe! I know how hard you've worked for this," I say, dropping a peck on his cheek, careful not to leave a lipstick smudge.

Not to be outdone, he wraps me in a bear hug.

"Ick." I squeal, "Get in the shower. You smell!"

He chuckles playfully as he reaches past me to turn on the shower faucet. A wicked look gleams in his eyes, but I shoot him a warning glare in response. Fortunately for me, he decides to play nice and release me.

As I scamper away, he calls out to me.

"Baby."

"Yes?" I say, looking over my shoulder.

"Thank you. I never could have gotten through any of this without you. The accident, my recovery, and everything we've been through this last year."

I smile softly at his earnest expression.

"You're my dream girl and the best mom in the world," he whispers, striding forward to drop a gentle kiss on my lips.

I sigh softly, but the wail of my daughter pierces the moment.

"I better go," I say, dropping my arms from his neck.

Walking into the dim room, I scoop up the crying infant and the bottle waiting on a nearby nightstand. As I sit in the old cane rocking chair that used to sit in my childhood home, I gaze up at the pastel pink walls and stenciled white daisies. My thoughts drift over how much has changed.

One year ago tonight, I found out I was pregnant. What followed was a long stretch of puking, anxiety, and so many frantic Google searches. But through it all, there was joy. Even though I struggled with fear the entire nine months, half convinced something horrible was going to go wrong, I didn't trap those feelings inside.

Shelby reminded me every day that things would get better, and spending time with Faith helped give me hope that it would all be worth it. Loyal Spencer held my hair every morning while I emptied the contents of my stomach, even though he turned a little green every time. Genie made me a special ginger tea that thankfully gave me some relief while Dad told me story after story of my mom's pregnancy and my early childhood.

The day I couldn't get my pants buttoned for the first time, I called Leslie and broke down crying on the phone. She dropped everything, drove to my house armed with an iced coffee, and took me shopping for maternity clothes. I have never felt more taken care of.

On a blazing hot August afternoon five months ago, every one of them was there waiting at the hospital for our tiny miracle to be born. At 7 pounds, 7 ounces, she made her world debut kicking and screaming. I have never felt so starstruck in my life. I couldn't speak. I couldn't cry. I just stared and whispered, "Hi, baby," over and over again like a mad woman.

It was the best moment of my life, and yet every day since has been equally rewarding. The days have not been without their share of challenges and parental fears. But somehow, I feel better prepared to handle them, thanks in part to the village that surrounds me.

A gurgling sound brings me back to the present.

"Well, if you're going to blow bubbles, baby girl, you must not be that hungry."

Her soft blue eyes crinkle as she flashes me a wide baby grin. I carry her to the changing table for a fresh diaper and dress her in a new Christmas dress. She lets out a string of babbles, and I make a face and tickle her belly.

"Can you say mama?" I sing-song.

"Da!" she shrieks and dissolves into giggles. This and peek-a-boo are her new favorite games.

"There's my little sweetie pie," Spence calls, stepping into the room still glistening from his shower.

She squeals and claps her hands together, babbling more nonsense.

Spencer scoops her up and gives her an exaggerated smooch on the cheek. It's no secret she's a daddy's girl, and I wouldn't have it any other way.

Turning to me, Spencer shoots me a wink, "Is everything ready? People are starting to arrive. I just saw Shelby pull up, and there's a guy with her."

"Perfect. She's been debating about inviting him for weeks. Glad I finally broke her down."

I slip past daddy and daughter and reach the front door in time to greet Shelby with a toddler on her hip.

"Hi, girlies," I say, pulling them both in for a tight hug.

"Tay Tay!" Faith exclaims.

Behind them, a man in dress slacks and a polo clears his throat uncomfortably as he holds up a casserole dish.

Shelby drops Faith to her feet, who quickly scampers off in search of her 'bay-bee.'

I have never seen my best friend look so nervous.

"Um, yeah, Taylor, this is Ryan."

The strikingly handsome face looks remarkably similar to…

"Wait. Ryan Heller?" I ask.

"Yeah. How'd you know?" Shelby says.

Recognition lights his eyes, "Yeah, you're Leslie's sister."

"Shelby," I say, thumping my friend's arm, "You didn't tell me Mr. Investment Banker was Leslie's brother-in-law."

Her mouth gapes slightly before she pulls her lips up into a smile. Spencer appears at my side.

"Ryan, hey! Nice to see you again, man." Spencer says, shaking his free hand, "Come on in, you guys. There's lots of food."

That's an understatement. Between Spencer's smoked meats, Genie's fresh homemade cookies, and the dozens of sides, desserts, and dips, there's enough food here to feed an entire army.

We all gather, and the din of various conversations rises through the room. Leslie and Peter show up, and more laughter is shared because, seriously, what are the odds that my best friend is falling for the brother of my sister's soul mate? It truly is a small world, and it seems everything is connected somehow.

Spencer's mom, Theresa, even makes a reluctant appearance. She is looking less haunted every time I see her, and sometimes, it pains me that I never made more of an effort to embrace my grieving mother-in-law all these years.

I'm convinced that there is something about a grandchild that fills that yawning ache. I've seen both her and my father transform these past few months. They have never seemed so young as they drop to the floor to shake a rattle or talk in a funny, high-pitched voice.

If my heart gets much bigger, it will surely split my chest in two.

I glance down to where my daughter and niece are playing with a ring stacker toy as Samuel looks on from the chair above them. I lift the mountain of white fluff and place him on my lap as I take a seat.

"Bay bee." Faith jabbers animatedly. "Baby hope."

"Yeah," I say, my heart squeezing, "You're right. That's baby Hope."

I look up to Shelby, who's sitting nearby with glistening eyes. "That's the first time she's ever said her name."

"I know," I say, amazed. "She's growing up so fast."

"She really is," Shelby says, "Hope and Faith. You know they're going to be best friends one day."

I chuckle softly, "Oh, but they already are."

A tinkling sound from the kitchen grabs our attention. Peter loops an arm around Leslie as he addresses the room.

"Leslie and I have an announcement to make. We got a call earlier today from the adoption agency, and a young pregnant woman has selected us to raise her child."

Emotion chokes his voice, and joyful tears stream down my sister's perfect features.

"In about six months, we're going to be parents," he says, almost in disbelief.

As congratulations echo around the living room, I reach Leslie first and pull her into a hug.

"I know it must be so overwhelming, but we'll all be here for you," I try to reassure her, but she still looks terrified.

"How am I going to do this?" she whispers, "I thought I'd have more time to prepare. They said it could take years to find a placement."

"Hey," I say, pulling back to meet her eyes, "Look around. The village is right here. We'll get through this."

She smiles through her tears as Genie, Dad, and Shelby line up to congratulate the new parents-to-be. Yes, Leslie and Peter will have no shortage of babysitters and familial support.

Ever the comedian, Spencer begins to laugh. I raise a questioning eyebrow at him.

"Well, you know if the baby is a girl, you'll have to name her Love," he gestures toward the giggling toddler and infant.

Ah, yes. Faith, Hope, and Love – The three most important gifts the world has been given

Everyone chuckles at his well-placed dad joke, but Leslie has a sudden dreamy look on her face.

"No," she says softly, "the love is already in this room."

Acknowledgments

I am incredibly grateful to my husband for lifting me up throughout our long journey toward parenthood and for allowing me to borrow pieces of our story as the inspiration behind *The Year Before Hope*. Thank you for being the Spencer to my Taylor, and for having my back through everything life throws our way.

To my beautiful best friend, Myranda — your insights and support have been incredible. Thank you for patiently following along as I sent this story to you, chapter by chapter, while it unfolded.

My entire work family at Daycos has been a godsend. I could not have written this book without a company culture that lifts each other up and supports personal growth. This book would not exist without you all. Special thanks to my cohort divas, my personal cheerleader, Melissa, and my go-to book-writing expert, Tammy.

To my coach, Paula — you helped me break through a wall in developing Taylor's character. Thank you for taking on my wild idea of coaching a fictional person.

To my developmental editor, Caroline Leavitt, thank you for your kind wisdom, thoughtful guidance, and words of encouragement. It was a joy to work with you.

My beta readers, you were phenomenal. Your thoughtful feedback helped shape the final version of this story, and I am deeply grateful.

Finally, I want to acknowledge my three children.

To the one I lost and grieved — I can't wait to meet you someday.

And to my two beautiful boys earthside. Thank you, from the bottom of my heart, for the joy and hope you bring me every single day.

About the Author

Angela K. Henery is a Nebraska-based author whose love for storytelling began the moment she learned to read and never really let go. Raised in a small town in the rural Midwest, she grew up surrounded by wide skies, quiet resilience, and stories worth telling.

After spending more than five years in journalism, Angela transitioned into communications and marketing, where she developed a deep appreciation for human-centered stories. While her professional path evolved, writing remained the constant thread. Her work evolved from short stories and a monthly outdoor column to books.

She wrote her first children's book after the birth of her oldest son, followed by a second a year later. Her debut novel, *The Year Before Hope*, marks a deeply personal and emotional chapter in her writing journey, exploring love, loss, and the strength it takes to keep going when life doesn't follow the plan.

When she's not writing, Angela can be found enjoying rainy

days, caramel lattes, romance novels, and time outdoors. Her books are dedicated to the three great loves of her life: her husband and her two sons.

You can connect with me on:

- https://www.angelakhenery.com
- Angela K. Henery
- @angela.k.henery

www.ingramcontent.com/pod-product-compliance
Lightning Source LLC
LaVergne TN
LVHW100528110826
845146LV00002B/815

* 9 7 9 8 2 1 8 9 1 8 7 4 3 *